Prologue

She *closed the lid of the suitcase and zipped it.*

Her car would be here in half an hour.

She sat at the dressing table, looking in the mirror. She looked haggard, she thought.

She was seething. Her expression was stoic, but fury bubbled inside her, threatening to erupt.

The call this morning had lasted only a few minutes. But it was the latest of many. And for her, the final straw.

No more, she vowed, staring into the mirror uncompromisingly.

It was time to stop this. Once and for all.

She glanced at the suitcase standing next to the door of her bedroom.

She had everything she needed.

She ran a mental inventory. One final check. It was a habit picked up when she started working so many decades ago. Do once, check twice.

One final look at the mirror. Then she took a deep breath and stood up.

Time to set things right. Permanently.

She grasped the handle of the suitcase and strode out of the door.

CHAPTER 1

Call me Ishmael.

Scratch that. Such a cheesy way to start *the* Great Singaporean Novel.

My name is Ishmael. Ishmael Dollah.

I am sixty years old.

I am a retired CEO.

Till about a year ago my serene life revolved around my wife, tennis, Netflix, Kindle and the club.

Then, I discovered that my daughter-in-law was having an affair with an asshole.

CHAPTER 2

I am a bit of an asshole myself. At least that is what my wife tells me when she ends our arguments.

'You are an asshole, Ishmael!'

Nysa uses other endearments too, but this is a frequent one.

I love her very much.

But I digress.

Yes, I know the first chapter seemed short.

It piqued your interest though, didn't it?

The first slide of your presentation has to provoke and excite rather than inform,' my first boss had repeated, a thousand times. *'the audience must lean forward in their seats in anticipation of what is coming next.'*

So as you saw, the first chapter hinted at money, sex, intrigue and a mysterious arch villain.

All the ingredients for a humdinger, you will agree?

'But,' my boss would continue, *'never promise what you cannot deliver. You cannot start the presentation with "Amazing First Quarter Results!" and then announce a miserly growth of 3 percent. The audience will feel let down, betrayed.'*

He is the reason why I disclosed only part of what is in store for you. This book has much more edge-of-the-seat, bite-your-nails-till-they-bleed stuff. But I have learnt, both from my boss and through experience that the surest path to customer satisfaction is to promise less and deliver more. So I will not reveal any more just yet.

'Next, share a little about yourself. Who you are, why you are here and what you are going to talk about,' were my boss' next instructions.

My name, as I said, is Ishmael Dollah.

I have no idea why my father insisted on naming me Ishmael. I had no say in the matter. Later, when I was old enough to recognise that this name was a millstone around my neck, I asked my mother why.

'He saw a movie,' she said, 'it had a big fish and a man with one leg. I don't remember the name. He liked it very much.'

I guess I am lucky he didn't name me Starbucks.

The origin of our last name, Dollah, is lost in the mists of time. It seems to appear frequently in Asia. There are many forms—Dola, Dolha, Dolah, Dowlah. It sounds vaguely Middle Eastern, but I could find no connection that crossed the Indian Ocean.

Our family has lived in South East Asia for the past six generations. We were originally farmers, then cultivators, then merchants and now white-collar workers. As far as I know, my ancestors belonged to the Adventist Church. I vaguely remember my grandparents taking me to church on Saturdays in Melaka, when I was a little child. This was before I could run faster than them.

My father was an accountant. He was a rigid, by-the-book, binary man. There was the right way, which was the way he did things, or the wrong way, which was any other way. He was not an easy man to live with. I believe both my mother and I felt, among other emotions, a sense of relief when he left us.

My mother was a teacher, a homemaker, an artist, a seamstress, a chef, a counsellor, a mediator, a confidante. She was the obverse of my father. My mother was the centre of our community, the first port of call and the court of last resort for our extended family and the entire neighbourhood.

I was an only child.

My childhood was one of silence. My father rarely spoke to me. It seemed like he never wanted to. My mother was busy all the time and spoke little to me, even if she wanted to. She looked after me, cared for me, gave me most of what I asked for. I knew she loved me. I loved her but did not really know her. So from early on, I engaged more with myself than I engaged with the world.

Because of this I learnt to watch and observe. While I never had it in me to sense emotions or feelings, I learnt to read and respond to them. Over time, I understood what people expected, what they wanted to see, and I fashioned my behaviour accordingly.

As I grew, I learnt to depend on no one but myself. I couldn't depend on my father, he was so remote. I couldn't depend on my mother, she was so involved.

I am an outcome of my father's strictures and my mother's nurture. This is not as easy as you think. I am often torn between discipline and freedom, rules and whims, right and acceptable. I have been stressed most of my life.

While these opposing forces were not great for my mental health, they worked well for my academics and career.

I did well in school, went on to study engineering, then spent a few years building and fixing things. I followed that up with a Master's in Management, then led teams that did various things such as marketing, selling and leasing, all focused on making money hand over fist.

My performance convinced my bosses to promote me at regular intervals. One day, I moved into a corner office as the CEO.

On my ascent up the corporate ladder, I have been called cold and calculating, ruthless and relentless. These are loose words from people who don't understand that once I decide my tasks and objectives, I ensure that I complete and achieve them, every single time. Failure may be the stepping stone to success, but I have always preferred to plan past failure rather than to step on it.

Life as a CEO, all fourteen years of it, was great. I built companies and transformed companies, turned them around and built a reputation of delivering amazing outcomes.

My first company as a CEO was Growstern Global, a family run company that we expanded across 15 countries within 6 years. The second was Biorgan, a public listed icon that had fallen on hard times; I turned this company around in 36 months and sold it to a hedge fund for a fortune. The third was Metrocyn, a transnational company that was stagnating and sliding towards obscurity; I transformed the group into the power house it is today.

Over the course of my career, I built a brilliant network of 'friends' and acquaintances, made quite a bit of money, and travelled the world.

'Don't go on and on till their eyes glaze over and they start nodding to sleep,' my boss had said when we overdid the 'about us' section with details no one was interested in.

Most of my life, I have tried my best to do the right things for the right reasons. As far as possible, I conformed to expectations. Even when it tore me apart, I trod the beaten path.

Time and again, I have suppressed the flares of rage and violence that erupted inside me when I observed people exploiting, hurting or dominating. I ignored and overlooked heinous behaviour. I inured myself from reacting to the deadly sins that humans repeatedly commit. I did this so that my family and I could lead a 'normal' life, a life that aligned with what society deems acceptable. So that the consequences of my actions would never hurt my wife or son.

However, since I retired about eighteen months ago, my life has taken a sharp turn into roads that most people haven't even seen, much less travelled.

My life has been thrown into turmoil. It is exciting and terrifying at the same time.

I feel like I am walking on the edge and could tip over into the abyss any time. But I don't want to stop.

I need to share this with someone. The pressure within me is too much to bear alone.

'Now, move into the main part of the presentation—the narrative,' my boss had continued, *'take the audience through the events that led to where you are today.'*

Thank you for joining me.

Please turn off your phones or put them on silent.

Please feel free to ask questions at any time.

CHAPTER 3

Coming back to the affair.

I would have never suspected Marianna of anything other than settling when she married Shahed. She was a ten, he was, at best, a seven. [Of course, she settled, Nysa!]

Till I attended her firm's annual Dinner & Dance last December.

Nestor & Ross threw some amazing parties, but their annual jamboree is to be attended to be believed.

The annual party was planned for the coming Thursday night. Shahed was traveling on work and could not attend. He was in KL, expected to be back only on Friday evening. Shahed has clients across South East Asia, so he travels 3-4 days a week.

Marianna had asked me to stand in for Shahed.

She had invited Nysa, too, but Nysa doesn't like big parties. Too loud, too many people, she says. Nysa prefers smaller groups.

I can take or leave parties, but as I said, the Nestor & Ross parties were awesome. Two years ago, they brought in David Copperfield, and he literally blew everyone's socks off. I am not joking—every single male in that party lost his socks. He refused to return them to us. By the time I reached home, I had a blister that took three days to subside. He still owes me sixteen dollars.

At 7 p.m. I picked up Marianna from their condo and drove to The Ritz-Carlton. This luxury hotel is located in the Marina Bay area, and is a favourite choice for corporate shindigs. They have great food and valet parking, two necessities for an enjoyable evening.

Marianna was about five and a half feet tall, just a couple of inches shorter than me. She was both slim and voluptuous, a combination most women would sell their husbands for. Her mixed ancestry made her features exotic, with a slight tilt to her eyes and a retroussé nose.

This evening, Marianna looked radiant in her turquoise blue off-shoulder dress. When we entered the ballroom foyer, most male heads swivelled. My head swelled.

Within a few minutes, Marianna had gotten swallowed up by groups of colleagues and friends, leaving me to make my way towards one of the four bars scattered in the foyer. I walked over to the furthest one, got myself a dark rum and Coke. And as was my usual practice, stood against the wall observing the crowd engage in their usual rituals.

You may have heard the phrase, 'Oh, I would have liked to be a fly on the wall in that room/during that meeting/ watching that argument.'

I was a fly on the foyer wall.

Sipping my drink, I looked and listened and smiled at the vagaries of humans.

In one group:

'Yeah, of course I know Martin. Smart guy, excellent lawyer, would have been a partner by now, except (lowering voice) for his body odour.'

'I know, it is impossible to sit next to him in the conference room! Hasn't he heard of deodorant?'

'Or a toothbrush?'

Chuckles and chortles all around.

In another group:

'You know, I felt so humbled to have received the award? I never dreamt that I would be recognised in this manner.'

'Is that the award, Jennifer, where one needs to nominate oneself and then ask friends to vote?'

A sudden snarl morphing into an indulgent laugh.

'Oh, Chetan, always the jester! You never stop pulling my leg, do you?'

Light, trilling laughter belied by angry, hate-filled eyes.

Then, two men walking past,

'...going to Bangkok next week. God, I love that place. The women, they are to die for ...'

'No, Justin, the women, they are to screw for!'

'Haha, well said! I really like the young ones, the ones who practically have no hair ...'

'I wish I was going with you ...'

Two glasses clinking together in celebration of mutual misogyny.

As I stood and watched and listened, now and again I glimpsed Marianna moving from this group to that, always the centre of attention.

After about 15 minutes, I walked to the bar to get a refill.

'Rum and Coke, eh?' said the man standing next to me, waiting for his drink. 'That is a classic that will never fade.'

He was of Chinese origin, wearing a snazzy designer suit sans the tie.

I smiled at him. 'Why change a winning combination?'

'Absolutely!' he grinned. He picked up his drink with his left hand and thrust his right at me. 'I'm James.'

'Ishmael,' I said, as we shook.

'Lawyer or client?' he asked, half joking.

I did not feel it necessary to explain my presence.

'Client.' I said.

'Welcome to Nestor & Ross,' said James, 'and thank you for your custom.'

We moved together to the wall and stood side by side. He seemed to be in his mid- to late-thirties but like many Chinese Singaporeans, could have been anywhere between thirty and seventy. They had hit the gene jackpot, remaining forever slim and youthful.

Over the next few minutes, James pointed out people and shared anecdotes about them. Some racy, some downright scandalous.

'That old man there, in the silver tie,' he said, leaning conspiratorially towards my ear, 'Roland Lum—he's under investigation by the CPIB for embezzlement. More than ten million dollars! I believe he has a mansion in Bintan and a beachfront property in Bali ...'

I nodded and sipped.

'And that one there, Chris Marshal,' he almost whispered, indicating an old white man with his head, 'on his third wife and fourth mistress—both of them share the same hairdresser!'

I wanted to yawn but did not. I was trained to be polite.

'Umm, I need to go and find …' I began, hoping to find a more peaceful stretch of wall.

'Ahh, the latest scandal of the season,' said James, ignoring my tentative plea, 'that woman in blue, Marianna— she and Greg Closier are steaming up her office windows "working late nights"!' He air-quoted the last three words and winked at me like an adolescent.

My wife says I have an expressive face. She is right. My team members would always be able to read my expressions easily. Especially those that did not bode well for them.

But I tried to keep my face blank. It helped that James was not looking at me—he was trying to spot his next news item.

'Who is Greg Closier?' I asked, as calmly as I could.

'Who? Oh, Greg? He is the Joint Managing Partner,' said James, 'I wouldn't be surprised if Marianna finds a promotion stuffed in her stocking this Christmas. Especially as he stuffs himself into her quite regularly!' He winked again, man to man.

'I see.' I resisted hitting James on his narrow skull with the heavy crystal glass in my hand.

'I wouldn't mind "stuffing" her myself,' he chuckled, air-quoting again, 'but I am too low in the pecking order. She doesn't even know who I am, probably.'

My resistance took on heroic proportions.

'It was a pleasure meeting you,' I said, levering myself off the wall. 'I have to find someone, it's quite important …'

James looked rather disappointed, after all I had been a willing foil for his commentary.

'A pleasure, Ishmael,' he said, 'hope to bump into you later this evening.'

I smiled, nodded and made my way around the small groups of chatter.

With a few words, James had shattered my comfortable world.

Marianna having an affair? Cuckolding poor Shahed? Our Marianna?

Shahed hit the jackpot when he wooed and married Marianna. They had met at a friend's party about twelve years ago. Nothing came out of that first meeting. They went their ways. They met again, by chance, at the wedding of a mutual friend a year or so later. They recognised one another from the party. When looking for their place cards, they realised that they were seated at the same table at the reception dinner. They sat next to each other. Over wine and then dinner, they spent the evening talking. That night changed their lives. From then on, they had eyes only for each other. Shahed proposed a few months later and their wedding took place soon after.

Marianna's family was originally from Penang in Malaysia. She came to Singapore about two decades ago to study and has lived here since, except for two years for her Master's in the UK.

Marianna is a lawyer, currently a partner at Nestor & Ross. She is an expert on corporate and contractual law.

I was quite surprised when Shahed and Marianna announced their engagement. Shahed was my son and I thought the world of him, but Marianna was clearly out of his league. Marianna was smart and talented, an editor of her college law review. She was ambitious—she wanted to run her own international law firm. She was drop-dead beautiful. Even though in her thirties, people approached her to model for them. Marianna could have had any man she wanted.

Was Greg Closier the man she wanted? Was she done with Shahed? Would she walk away, leaving him bereft and broken?

The star of the evening's entertainment was Russel Peters. He had everyone laughing till they were rolling in the aisles. I sat still, unaffected by the gales of laughter erupting around me.

Interlude 1 – Nysa, Concerned

Something is wrong with Ishmael.

Since last week he has been morose and glum. However much I try and talk to him, all I get in return are monosyllables and grunts. It is not as if he was a great conversationalist in the first place, but normally he at least listens and engages. Now, he is on a different planet altogether. All remote and isolated.

I know this started with Marianna's party. Yes. I am sure of it. He came back that evening and didn't speak to me, just went directly to his study. He didn't say anything about the party—the food or the decorations or the entertainment. He knows I love hearing about such stuff, and he usually describes them in detail.

Then, the next morning, he actually slept late and did not go for his morning run. The last time this happened was when he had high fever and could not even get up from bed! I remember we had to go to the doctor who prescribed a course of antibiotics and bed rest. Ha—Ishmael went for his run the next morning.

I am worried. I have known Ishmael for nearly forty years. Every time he has been in such a mood, he has lashed out.

I remember the time when he thought that our neighbour, Herman, was hitting on me. All he did, poor man, was bring me some flowers that he had received when he opened his new store. I know Ishmael followed him and beat him up behind the carpark. I am not a fool, you know. I understand what split knuckles and bleeding lips mean. After that day, Herman avoided me like the plague till we moved out of that condo. I didn't know whether to laugh or cry. Whether I should feel safe or scared. It was all so silly, and so macho.

Then, I remember the time when Shahed was being bullied at school. By that stupid ang moh boy, Benjamin, who was two years older and twice Shahed's size. Big bully! I remember Ishmael going all quiet and grim. And then, a week later Benjamin was pulled out of the school by his parents. After that we never heard anything about him or his parents. I don't have any proof, but I am sure Ishmael had something to do with that.

Ishmael is always protective of his family. Sometimes a little more than he needs to be, I think. But what is the problem this time? Did someone behave improperly with Marianna? Or say something disrespectful? Is Ishmael going to beat someone up again? He is sixty, for God's sake; what happens if he gets beaten up?

Or could it be something completely different?

Could he have met someone at the party? Someone younger and slimmer and sexier? He still looks lean and sexy and distinguished. And he is still so full of energy. I have seen how women look at him, even though he has no clue. Last month, at the Halloween party, that cow Sarah was oozing all over him. Touching him unnecessarily and laughing at everything he said, as if he was Trevor Noah. Awful cow!

I know I have let myself go these past few years. I used to fit comfortably into 'small', now anything less than 'large' is a tight fit. I know Ishmael still says I am beautiful, but I know he is just saying it to make me feel good. I feel fat and frumpy.

Just last year, Garima's husband left her for a thirty-year-old colleague in his office. After twenty-five years of marriage! Now, she lives alone in Johor Bahru, just about making ends meet while he and his new wife are living in Nassim Road and expecting a baby. Poor thing. And Garima is still slim and pretty. Unlike me.

Is Ishmael tired of me? I know we haven't been making love as much as we used to. My research work has also increased, so much that we are spending much less time together than we used to. Does he feel neglected?

What should I do?

I know I must get back to exercising regularly. But my knees hurt. And it is so boring. My trainer keeps telling me that I should at least walk five kilometres every day. I need to listen to him. I will start tomorrow. Not, not tomorrow, I have a lot of work, I'll start next week. Yes, I will. And I will cut down on sweets—no more bedtime snacking. Also, I haven't waxed for a long time. I must set up an appointment asap.

How can I get Ishmael to tell me what the problem is? How can I get him to confide in me?

I will just be nicer and more cheerful. And I'll be a better listener. I know I am much more impatient with him than I am with Siti or Shahed or anyone else. I know I take Ishmael for granted.

Am I pushing him away without even knowing? Am I going to end up like Garima? God, I hope not.

I can't live in Johor Bahru ...

CHAPTER 4

'What is the matter with you?' asked Nysa impatiently. 'Why are you moping around?'

I looked at her. After 35 years of marriage, she was still the most beautiful woman I had ever seen. Granted, there was a lot more of Nysa than when we first got married. She likes food and loathes exercise. But she still sparkled and glowed. Her presence warmed me. Nysa was the reason that my life had not imploded. Her light has steadfastly guided me through the dark.

Right now, her trademark smile was absent, and her trademark furrowed brow was front and centre. She sensed something was wrong and wanted to know what and why.

'Nothing,' I said, as nonchalantly as I could, 'I am fine.'

'No, you are not!' she shot back, 'Something is bothering you, and you are bottling it up as you always do. What is it?'

'Nothing,' I repeated, 'Just some issues with our investments that I need to sort out.' I rose from the dining table where we had just finished our afternoon tea. 'I am going down to the FairPrice to buy cigarettes. Do you need anything?'

'No, thanks,' she said, as she rose. She looked at me. 'But you already have cigarettes on your shelf.'

'I bought the wrong ones,' I said, 'Be back soon.'

I could feel her eyes on my back as I left the dining room.

The last week had been hellish.

Five days had passed since the Nestor & Ross party.

Every day was agonising.

I was used to solving problems, fixing situations. I had spent a decade and a half as a CEO doing just that, and doing it well.

But this situation was new to me.

Don't get me wrong. I have encountered affairs before. Every company I worked in had someone or the other who couldn't keep it in their pants, or couldn't keep their panties on. I have never understood this desperate desire to sleep with someone that one works with. That is like drinking Scotch while eating cake. Ugh.

I have had to counsel and warn, and sometimes, terminate.

In my last company, Metrocyn, the CFO and the Vice President of HR were found compromising themselves in various positions in diverse hotels. That in itself was not the problem—they were both consenting adults, even though they were adulterous consenting adults. The problem was that the VP of HR was sharing a lot of confidential information, including the terms of my contract, with the CFO, which was a breach on both their parts.

I fired both of them for cause, with complete prejudice, and reported them to the Stock Exchange. I did what I had to do without qualms or regrets.

This was different.

This was our Marianna, for God's sake. Our daughter! How could she betray Shahed? How could she do this to Nysa and me?

The previous Sunday, Marianna and Shahed had come over for dinner, as they regularly did. I wasn't sure if I would be able to deal with it. How could I sit across Marianna, knowing she was cheating on my son and not allow it to show on my face and in my bearing? So, I invented an old friend who I said was visiting town, and who wanted to have dinner at the Club. I then left before Marianna and Shahed arrived and stayed out till I was sure they had left.

Nysa was not amused. She gave me the silent treatment for almost twenty-four hours before she relented. She was still snippy and huffy, but at least she was talking to me.

My walk extended to beyond the FairPrice store. I kept walking as my thoughts kept churning. I had to do something. But what?

As I walked, I realised that I was reverting to type. When I was working, and when I faced a problem, I would leave my car in the office and walk back home. The hour and a half alone with my thoughts allowed me to focus on the problem, on alternate solutions, on fitting and testing each solution and evaluating outcomes. Most often, by the time I reached home, I had found a workable fix. Yes, I had to take a cab to work the next day, but that was a small price to pay.

As I crossed the five-kilometre mark, my thoughts gradually started unravelling from the knotted mess that they were and forming into bullet points.

I had to save my son's marriage.

To do this:

First, I had to confirm the truth of James' allegations. Yes, he had no reason to lie but was there really fire, or was he just blowing smoke?

Second, if James' words were true, I would need to find a way to separate Marianna and Greg. How?

Third, even if Marianna and Greg ceased their unholy dalliance, what about Marianna and Shahed? Would they recover from such a betrayal?

Finally, I had to do this myself. I could not involve anyone else. Our family was at stake. Did I have the bandwidth?

Bullet points are usually great clarifiers, but these did little to mitigate my angst.

As I retraced my way back, I considered diverse approaches. Some I rejected outright. A few I parked for later analysis. One or two, I thought, were possibles.

Each of them needed further thought, and if found viable, required a whole lot of planning and preparation.

It would also require me to travel well beyond my comfort zone. I would need to gird myself to do things and take risks I would not have condoned in the past. I have, at certain junctures, bent rules to breaking point.

Like almost every CEO. This time, I may need to break them with impunity. And without the might or money of an organisation backing me.

Well, I thought as I walked back into our lobby, *I have a set of options to analyse, decisions to make and actions to take.*

I put on my game face and entered our apartment.

It was almost dinner time. I went to our bathroom, washed up and changed into fresh, clean clothes.

Then, I went to the kitchen where Nysa was putting the finishing touches to one of her world-famous desserts.

I leaned against the door as rakishly as I could.

'Hey sweetheart, I am back,' I said.

Nysa looked up. She seemed to be in a better mood. That was the great thing about Nysa. She could never stay angry with me for long. Or with anyone else for that matter. She was, by default, a daughter of light. She never allowed gloom to linger.

'Ready for dinner?' she asked.

'Yes, and I am starving.' I said, as piteously as I could.

'Could you take the rice and egg curry to the table?' she asked, 'I'll just finish this and be with you.'

I did as she requested, and laid out the table mats and cutlery, as a bonus.

At dinner, I took special effort to be my normal self. I asked Nysa about her research, and she told me about how different foods travelled across the world through history, changing and impacting traditional cuisines. She shared examples of a few 'national cuisines', considered traditional dishes handed down generations, which were actually very recent inventions. They were just marketed brilliantly, creating a strong impression on public consciousness.

I listened, nodded and laughed.

After clearing the table and washing up, we sat holding hands and watched one of the *Fast and Furious* movies. I can't remember which one—I only know it was the one where Gal Gadot gets thrown out of a plane.

What a waste. They should have thrown out Vin Diesel instead.

As the credits rolled, I excused myself.

'Sorry, Nysa, I need to review a couple of documents,' I said, 'Is that okay?'

'Of course, Ishmael,' said Nysa, 'I, too, need to complete the last few chapters in the book I am researching. I should be done in an hour or so.'

I kissed her hand and went to the study.

I sat down at my desk and opened my laptop. I pulled out the pens and pencils in my pen stand. Three of the four pens had dried a lingering death. Both the pencils were more blunt than a bread knife. I threw the dry pens into the dustbin and sharpened the pencils. I checked the paper in the printer. I got up and shut the door to the study, something I hadn't done for a long while.

I was reverting to an older version of me that I had thought was archived. I noticed that while the pain from Marianna's betrayal still lingered, it was now overlaid by a sense of anticipation.

Something that had been coiled inside me, lying dormant these past months, was stirring.

CHAPTER 5

I reached into the bottom drawer of my desk and pulled out a notepad that I hadn't used for eighteen months.

It was my 'to-do' notebook, the one I used to organise my thoughts on any important project when I was working.

It still had about thirty pages left.

I opened the book to the first blank page.

This is what I wrote —

Step 1:
To confirm the allegations.
1. *How can I confirm the allegations beyond doubt?*
2. *What resources do I have at my disposal?*
3. *What tactics best fit this situation?*

That part was easy.

But answering the three questions was not as straightforward.

I leaned back in my chair and allowed my thoughts to roam.

If Marianna and Greg are having an affair, I surmised, they are having it outside the office.

This was not a random guess. I have been to the Nestor & Ross office. It is mostly an open plan, even the partners' cabins have clear glass walls. Unless they frequented the janitor's closet, it is unlikely that their intimacies took place in the legal equivalent of an Apple store.

So, to find where they were having the affair, I needed to know where they went, how long they stayed and how they explained themselves.

While Nysa and I are big fans of private detective dramas that revolve around finding the bad guys, I had no idea how to even start.

Being clueless was not new to me.

Four times in my career I have been parachuted into departments or companies I had no clue about and been asked to rescue or transform them.

The first time was on a Friday afternoon when I was asked to take over the warehousing and logistics department of Axxon. This was in the dark days before Amazon, smart phones and RFID tags. I had a vague, layman's idea of how warehouses worked, how goods were transported and delivered. The incumbent manager was demoted and left in a huff, without handing over any documents.

I was told by the sales teams—we had five of them for different product lines—that more than fifteen consignments had to leave on Monday.

Half an hour after being handed over this poisoned chalice, I searched through my Rolodex (an ancient artifact that held one's contacts in physical form) and found an acquaintance in a logistics company. I called him and explained the situation and asked him for help. He was a sweetheart and agreed without hesitation.

I spent Friday night, the whole of Saturday and part of Sunday getting a crash course on how goods were received, sorted, stored, picked, packed and despatched while ensuring that tens of documents were filled, approved, signed and filed.

On Sunday afternoon, I went to the Axxon warehouse. There I met a warehouse officer whom I had requested to come over with the promise of a compensatory day off. Together, we collated the fifteen sales orders, identified the consignments, tagged them and completed the documentation. While doing this, I called our transport contractors, disturbing them at dinners, movies and birthday parties.

On Monday morning, many of my colleagues watched, anticipating my epic failure. But at 10 a.m., the first trucks rolled in. By 3 p.m., all fifteen consignments were loaded and on their way to destinations flung far and wide.

Success, I learnt that day, was not about having years of experience. It was about having the appropriate knowledge. Most people confuse the two and pay dearly for that mistake.

Now, I had to find a way to track Marianna and Greg, and identify where they went, when and for how long.

This was not a topic that I could easily broach with a friend or passing acquaintance.

So I opened Google and typed, 'How do I track someone's location?'

In 0.007 seconds, Google spat out 487,000 results.

Wow.

Over the next hour, I roamed a world that I knew existed but had never really visited.

Did you know that you don't have to be James Bond to have cool gadgets that track people?

Did you know that you can read all Sent and Received text messages on someone's phone with the right app?

Did you know that you can read and monitor all their social media activity on Instagram, Viber, Snapchat, Telegram, WhatsApp and what have you?

All this for less than 5 Sing dollars a month?

Yes, there were some not so exotic, easily available trackers—RFID trackers and GPS trackers that were meant to track children and animals. But they did not really do everything I wanted them to do. They allowed one to locate but did not offer a record of movement.

I was looking for something more intrusive.

I continued my research till almost 11 p.m.

I evaluated six different apps, read reviews, compared specifications and offers.

Finally, I chose one. No, I am not going to tell you which one. For now, let's call it 'Tracker'.

I was itching to move forward, but I had ignored Nysa enough. So I closed my laptop and went to the bedroom.

'Finally,' she said when she saw me, 'where have you been? What are you doing?'

'Oh, I just needed to research some information for a mentee,' I said, 'he has a new business idea and I was checking the internet for possible competitors and prospective customers.'

'I am watching *The Crown*,' she said, then asked, 'Would you like to watch something else?'

'No, I am quite tired,' I said, 'you continue watching, I'll probably drop off to sleep.'

I nodded off to the sounds of the Queen and Prince Philip arguing about how they had grown apart. The Queen seemed distraught. I knew exactly how she felt.

The next morning, I arose half hour earlier than usual.

I washed, dressed and went for my run, starting on Orchard Road, transiting to Tanglin Road and then continuing along the Alexandra Canal to Queensway. I turned around near Ikea and started on my way back when it started to rain.

The rain energised me. My strides became longer and my pace faster. I pounded past people scurrying under umbrellas and hiding under awnings. I felt free.

When I entered our condo, the security guard looked at me from inside his cosy nook as if I were insane. I smiled and waved at him to reinforce that perception.

On entering our apartment, I went straight to the study and undressed. Two minutes later, a pulsing jet of scalding water was massaging and warming me.

I have no idea why people sleep in, when they could be running in the rain.

'So, what's the plan today?' asked Nysa, as we were having breakfast.

'I have some chores that I need to do,' I said. 'Then I will be playing tennis in the evening at the Club.'

'I am going for a study group meeting,' said Nysa. 'Do you need the car?'

Nysa is part of a forum called the Singapore Study Group. It consists of about thirty people who love learning. They agree on topics every twelve weeks. Each week, two members of the group present a detailed thesis on the topic either at one of the members' residences or on Zoom. The topics are wide ranging. One was about the impact of spices on civilisation. Another was on unsung women heroes. I attend as many as I can. Some of the presentations were absolutely fascinating.

'No, I will be around, you go ahead,' I said, as we cleared the table.

Fifteen minutes later, I said bye to Nysa and walked to Lucky Plaza on Orchard Road. This is an anomaly on Orchard Road. Most malls like Ion and Ngee Ann City and Paragon are high end, stuffed with designer showrooms and stores that extract small fortunes from the unwary. Lucky Plaza was more like a 'workers' mall'. It had currency exchange, money transfer, phone repair, 3-for-5 dollar products, and discount stores. It stood there, thumbing its nose at the sneering dowagers and had more customers per square foot than the other three malls combined. Lucky Plaza is a confusing place with sudden turns and unexpected cul de sacs.

At one small shop, I bought a low end Oppo phone. In the next shop, I bought a Simba SIM card.

I returned to our apartment and went into the study. I put the phone to charge and inserted the SIM card. Then I downloaded Tracker on the phone. I learnt how to make sure there was no icon visible on the screen.

While the Oppo phone was charging, I downloaded the app on my own phone.

I spent about an hour exploring all the features and getting accustomed to toggling between screens and menus.

Then I put both phones to charge, strolled to the kitchen and asked our helper, Siti, for a light lunch.

After lunch, I watched TV while waiting for Nysa to return from her meeting.

Nysa returned at 2 p.m. While she had her lunch, she told me about the presentations in the study group. While I am normally spellbound during her recitations, I was a little distracted today. I gathered that the current topic was 'Icons and Symbols in Asia'. One of the presentations was on the Swastika. I didn't recall the other one at all mainly because Nysa was quite scathing about the presenter's numerous gaffes and errors.

'Why don't people prepare properly, Ishmael?' she asked, in an affronted voice, 'Why do they take things so casually?'

I made appropriate soothing noises, and agreed with her that such people should spend an eternity in the hottest corner of hell. Then I took my leave, claiming to do some chores. I took both the phones and drove across Singapore—first to Marina Bay Sands, then to Siglap Road, from there to Terminal 1, onward to Eunos, then to Mandai Road, from there to Lentor Avenue, and finally back home. Fifty-two kilometres.

In our apartment, I holed up in my study and checked the Tracker on my phone.

I was both thrilled and horrified.

Every stop, every trip was logged.

It was almost as if a satellite was tracking me everywhere I went.

The app timed each stop and each trip to the microsecond. Not only could I see where the phone went, I could see how long it spent there.

I now knew how to track them.

I just had to overcome a small problem. I had to get Tracker onto Marianna's phone.

Segue 1 – Ishmael's Notebook

— *November:*

Task 1:
To confirm the allegations.

    1.   *How can I confirm the allegations?*
    2.   *What resources do I have at my disposal?*
    3.   *What tactics best fit this situation?*

Follow on notes:

    1.   *Confirming the allegations?*
        a.   *Track Marianna's movements.*
        b.   *See where she goes other than office.*
        c.   *Note how long she stays there.*
        d.   *Cross-check with her about her day and correlate her answers with her movements.*
        e.   *Check if Greg's movements mirror Marianna's????*
    2.   *Resources?*
        a.   *The Tracker app, for now.*
        b.   *My relationship with Marianna and Shahed.*

   c. No shortage of funds.
   d. No problem about time.

3. Tactics?

   a. Extreme caution. Nysa cannot find out.
   b. Outside office space—I need to move around without explaining myself each time.
   c. Dark browser.

CHAPTER 6

How do I place the Tracker app on Marianna's phone?

First, I would have to get my hands on her phone. Then, I would need to access her phone (I have no idea what her password is, and whether it's fingerprint or facial recognition). Finally, I would have to load the Tracker app and hide it.

If I were a 'white hat' or a 'black hat' or any kind of hacker, I would do this with consummate ease and grace. But I don't wear hats. I can't use my own phone without needing help, leave alone figuring out someone else's.

This needed some thought.

I called out to Nysa, 'Sweetheart, I am going out for a walk, see you in an hour or so!'

On hearing her response, I changed into my running gear and set out to find a solution.

My normal route includes Orchard Road, Tanglin Road, Napier Road, the Botanic Gardens and Bukit Timah Road. It is a pleasing mix of light and nature, of crowds and calm.

Today, I decided to reverse my usual route. I walked into the Botanic Gardens from the Bukit Timah entrance, savoured the cool, fresh air of the Gardens, then walked towards Orchard.

Twenty minutes later, I walked past Lucky Plaza. Then I stopped. On a whim, I retraced my steps and walked into the mall.

I looked for a cell phone repair shop. Ah, there was a small shop at the end of the corridor. Its numerous signs promised excellence, satisfaction and speed.

Thankfully, there were no customers awaiting service.

'Good evening, sir,' I said to the young man at the counter, 'may I trouble you for some help?'

'Hello, Uncle,' he said cheerfully. In Singapore, if you were male and had a smidge of grey hair, you were an 'uncle'. 'Of course, tell me.'

'If my phone is not working, and I have to give it for repair, can I transfer all the data into another phone temporarily?' I asked.

'What phone?' he asked.

'iPhone,' I said, equally tersely.

'Can can lah! If your data is on iCloud,' he said confidently. 'Then no need to transfer, only need to download.'

'If Samsung, then?' I asked.

'Samsung, also, I think,' he said, but not as confidently as before.

I nodded my head.

'Thank you so much,' I said, gratefully.

'No problem, uncle,' he said.

Two hours later, I returned with a hopeful spring in my step, went straight to my study, opened the laptop and the browser.

Fifteen minutes later, I had confirmed what the young man had said to me.

I sat back and smiled.

I had figured out how to get the Tracker app on Marianna's phone.

As a bonus, during my search, I'd also found some very useful information.

One, how to use a phone as a basic GPS tracker.

Two, how to ensure that such a phone can be left in place without it running out of charge for at least a week.

Both these were useful pieces of information. It occurred to me that I may need to track either Marianna's or Greg's car. Using a cheap phone to do so would achieve the objective without causing suspicion in the event of it being found.

I opened my notebook and wrote in it, leaving damp marks on the page and the table around it.

Then I went and had a long hot shower as a reward for my awesomeness.

As I was drying myself, Nysa summoned me for dinner. I was glad as I needed to suck up to her a little.

'Hi, Nysa,' I said, as I walked into the dining room, 'I am hungry enough to eat the crockery. What's for dinner?'

'Pomelo salad,' she said, 'followed by Quattro Formaggi Pizza.'

'Wow,' I said, sitting down, 'that sounds delicious.'

'Followed by Black Forest cake,' she ended on a high note.

I gorged on the food without any urging. Pomelo salad is a dish designed by and for the gods. Pizza is a dish designed by and for Italians. The rest of us eat cake.

Between courses, I paused.

'Darling, when are we seeing the kids next?' I asked Nysa, as casually as possible.

'The day after tomorrow, Saturday afternoon,' she replied. 'Why? Are you planning on meeting another friend?'

Nysa has a very good memory, and very little diffidence when it comes to stating her mind.

'No, I am feeling terrible that I wasn't there last week, and am looking forward to catching up,' I said, as earnestly as I could.

Nysa looked at me. She knew something was not right.

'What is going on, Ishmael?' she asked, earnestly. I couldn't read her expression. She seemed both worried and wary.

I put on my blandest face.

'Nothing,' I said, with as much sincerity as I could feign, 'why do you ask?'

'Something has changed since you came back from that party last week,' said Nysa. 'You have been all grumpy and moody. You are going off on walks at all times of the day. What is it? I feel that you are keeping something from me.'

I should have known better than to assume that Nysa would overlook the sudden change in my demeanour. She has boatloads of empathy and can smell a raw emotion from a mile away.

'Oh, Nysa,' I said, as if glad to get it off my chest, 'it is nothing to do with the party. On Friday, I got a call saying that Mohan, a friend from college, has been diagnosed with cancer and is terminal. A few of us have been trying to put together a fund for him and his family.'

Nysa's hand went to her mouth. Her face changed, from wary to sad.

'Oh, I am so sorry to hear that,' she said, 'why didn't you tell me?'

'What is the point of making you also unhappy, dearest,' I said, the lies flowing smoother than eighteen-year-old scotch, 'especially when there is nothing that you or I can do.'

I continued to tell her about Mohan and his fictitious disease, his family and the imaginary pain they were all in. Of this, only Mohan was real, and as far as I know, fit as a fiddle.

We finished dinner and cleared the table together as usual. I helped with washing up as Nysa and Siti put away the food.

As I was leaving the kitchen, Nysa hugged me and kissed me hard.

I glanced askance at her.

She just shook her head and smiled. She seemed relieved, which puzzled me. My lies about Mohan and the pain his family was going through warranted a different outcome, I thought.

I went to the study and reviewed everything I had learnt that day. Over the years, I had realised that a quick revision after absorbing something new fixes it firmly in my mind. During the review, a couple of questions arose, which Google kindly answered. I shut the laptop and went to the bedroom.

Nysa was there already, preparing for bed.

I looked at her admiringly and said, 'You look really beautiful tonight, dearest. Is that a new nightie?'

She smiled and preened a little. I am usually a klutz, but I have my moments.

She came to me and kissed me again. I took her in my arms. We continued kissing. While we were doing so, the nightie somehow, of its own volition, slithered to the floor.

I slept the sleep of the sated that night.

CHAPTER 7

I arose earlier than usual the next morning.

It was Friday and it promised to be a busy day.

It was dark and Nysa was still asleep when I set out on my run. The pavements were empty, as were the streets. As I ran in and out of the pools of light from the streetlamps, I reviewed my plan for the day.

Purchases, testing, research, review.

By the time I turned around, I was running into the rising sun, my t-shirt darkening with sweat and my skin darkening with melanin. By the time I reached our condo, I was drenched and tanned. I went to the study and switched on the AC. The cool air felt like an infusion of plasma.

'Hey, Nysa,' I said over breakfast, half hour later, gulping down my flavoured yoghurt, 'I have a discussion with a prospective client at 9.30 a.m. at the club. They are looking for someone to mentor their management team,'

'Oh, that's nice!' smiled Nysa. 'What does the company do?'

'They are a scale-up, developing apps for the F&B domain,' I said, lying through my omelette. 'Growing quite fast and noticing structural problems as they expand.'

'Now, don't go and say that you will work for free!' Nysa cautioned. 'You are doing enough of that. If this company is growing, that means they should be able to pay for your time!'

'We haven't discussed terms yet,' I said, 'Let's see how the discussions progress.'

'Will you be back for lunch?' she asked.

'Not sure, sweetheart,' I replied. 'I don't know how long the meeting will last and whether it will extend into lunch. I will keep you posted. Is it okay if I take the car? Do you need it for anything?'

'No, I am at home today,' she said, 'I need to complete my study group presentation for next week. There is a ton of research I need to do.'

'All the best, dearest,' I said, as we returned the dishes to the kitchen and wiped the table clean.

I set out at 9 a.m. I carried the Oppo phone I had purchased the previous day.

I drove first to Orchard Road and parked in Lucky Plaza. I went into the mall for the third time in two days and bought two more SIM cards and one more Oppo phone.

From there, I walked three hundred metres to the Apple store, where I bought the iPhone 14 for a small fortune.

I went back to Lucky Plaza and drove to the club, where I sat in one corner of the Reading Room, and assembled the phones and tested them. I loaded Tracker onto both new phones, and another app that Tracker recommended I load alongside.

An hour later, I left the club taking all three phones on a nice long drive, stopping at different points for different lengths of time (and timing the stops), and returned to the club at lunchtime.

While having lunch in the All-Day Coffee Shop (again in a dimly lit corner), I checked the Tracker app's robustness on all three phones. The app worked magnificently. I doffed a mental hat to the creator of the app—that was one cool and dangerous dude.

I continued sitting in the club, doing something I should have done before—extracting as much information from the internet about Nestor & Ross and Greg Closier as I could.

I knew very little about both.

Ninety minutes later, after entering and exiting LinkedIn, Facebook, Instagram and Google, I knew more, but not enough. I needed to do more research, using different tools than I had used so far. I saved the files that I had downloaded into a password-encrypted folder. I would review them again.

I returned home by 4 p.m. and tucked away the phones carefully. I was not in the mood to answer questions on why I had four phones, when I couldn't operate even one properly.

I am not very sensitive to moods and emotions. I can rarely read the room, and when I do, it is mostly wrong.

For the past forty years, every performance appraisal of mine has had the terms, 'task-focused', 'goal-oriented', 'achieves promised results' or variations thereof inscribed by bosses, peers and subordinates. This sounds positive but these are polite phrases that essentially mean—Ishmael 'puts tasks ahead of people', 'prioritises goals over teams' and is 'a pit bull who will try and win at all costs'.

In short, *not* a people's person.

But even I, from last evening's conversation at dinner, had realised that my anxiety and worry had driven me inward. I wasn't spending enough time with Nysa and, more importantly, my behaviour was triggering her suspicion and concern. And that would not do.

The story about Mohan was necessary but not sufficient. I needed to put in more work on ensuring that Nysa was on even keel again.

'Nysa, may I have the pleasure of your company for dinner tonight?' I asked when I reached home and kissed her.

She smiled prettily and said, 'Yes, sweetheart, I would love that!'

I called and booked a table at Nysa's favourite Greek restaurant.

We spent the rest of the afternoon watching a sitcom about a Korean family in Canada running a convenience store. We went through three episodes till it was time to leave for dinner.

We arrived at Blue Santorini at 6.45 p.m.

It was a gorgeous little restaurant run by a Greek family, who treated us like their own. We didn't even need to order—they knew what Nysa liked and what I didn't, and the dishes appeared as if by magic.

I spent most of dinner lying to Nysa about my 'meetings' and the consultancy project I was likely to be awarded. When I had exhausted that topic we spoke about our plans for Thanksgiving, Christmas and New Year's Eve. We ate, laughed and teased.

I reiterated that last week was an anomaly due to the news about Mohan. That everything was just fine. That there was no need to worry, and that if I had any issues I would immediately confide in her, as I always have.

Nysa bought my narrative. I think.

When we returned home, we seemed to be back on track. Nysa resumed her research on food migration. I went to the study and resumed my search for information.

I made another note—learn how to clear my browser history and ensure no trace of my stalking remained in my laptop.

As I delved deeper, what was grainy and blurred from my searches in the afternoon gradually sharpened and fleshed out. I was able to access the entire organisation chart of Nestor & Ross and discern the different teams, including Greg's team, which included Marianna and eight other lawyers and paralegals. I had been able to put together a rough roster of their clients. Their news section happily shared every little achievement and I got a good idea of their activities and priorities.

The profile of Greg Closier was also taking shape. However, this was slow progress as I was spending less time on Greg and more time trying to identify what Marianna's role was, where Marianna would normally go and where she would not. This helped me in spotting anomalies in her behaviour while tracking her movements.

As I was dove deeper and deeper, a feeling of déjà vu swept over me.

Remember we spoke about 'appropriate knowledge' a couple of chapters ago?

A few years earlier, I was asked to take over the marketing and sales for Axxon. While theoretically I boasted of a post graduate degree in marketing management, I had never worked in marketing ever.

So, I fell back on my mantra. I learned. From colleagues, from friends in other companies, from books, videos, seminars and conferences. I packed four years of college into three months.

Thereafter, every time I was targeting a customer, I would spend hours, even days, researching the customer organisation, their top people, their stated and unstated aspirations, so that I could find the right levers to influence and persuade. The effort, which many of my colleagues derided as unnecessary, always paid off, in spades.

I am doing this again. Absorbing everything I can so that I can find the right levers.

What goes around, comes around, one way or the other.

By 11 p.m., I found that I was yawning more than I was reading.

I shut everything down and conducted a final review for the next day. Did I have everything? Was I clear about my plan? And my back up plan?

Sort of satisfied, I decided to call it a night. I was tired. Being sixty may instil some wisdom in one's head, but it sure is hell on the body.

Interlude 2 – Marianna, Excited

What is wrong with me?

I am constantly excited. Constantly aroused.

Ever since Greg and I started meeting, I am unable to sit calmly or focus on my work.

Yes, I know, there is so much at stake.

Sometimes I wonder why I am taking this risk. I have a good life. It's comfortable, it's happy, it's stable. It is progressing steadily in all respects.

But I have never felt this way before. Never before have I taken such a leap into forbidden territory. Never before have I been on the cusp of breaking all norms and traditions. Never before have I been so aflutter and agog.

Even when I was dating Shahed, even when I knew he was going to propose, I was much more poised.

I think this is going to change everything, that's why.

Yes, I can see an amazing future Greg and I can build together. But I wasn't born with a silver spoon like him. My values are still firmly embedded in the middle class. Taking such a step goes against everything I was brought up with, everything I was taught was acceptable.

But there is no doubt that Greg and I are great together. We mesh perfectly. We bring out the best in each other.

There is so much to plan and so much to do.

And all this without Shahed knowing. He is an innocent, he will never find out till it's a done deal. Also, he is always travelling and has no clue what is going on around him.

I haven't told Dad anything either. He lives in his own world of golf, fishing and his book club. I don't think he will approve, but he will support me, whatever decision I take.

That leaves Nysa and Ishmael.

Nysa is a sweetheart. She doesn't probe or pry. I will tell her when the time comes. But Ishmael is a different cup of tea. I think he suspects something. Ever since the party—God, did he hear something there? But no one knows about Greg and me, so he couldn't have.

I wish I could speak to someone. I normally confide in Su Yee and Janice, but I can't speak to them about this. Janice, especially, will surely tell Philip, who will tell Pauline. I can't take the risk.

All this secrecy and tip-toeing around is making me tingle. Everything they said about forbidden fruit turned out to be right.

Gosh, is it hot in here!

The aircon is on full blast. It must be me. I can't sleep. I am too excited. I need some release.

Where is my vibrator?

Oh, here it is. I hope the damn thing works; I haven't used it for so long.

Aah, it works.

Aah, yes, it works …

CHAPTER 8

Saturday morning began like most Saturdays—with two hours of tennis at the club, a short run and extreme exhaustion thereafter.

The tennis games today were slower than usual. One of our regular foursome was travelling, and the replacement was not as quick, or as accurate.

The run was to ensure that I burnt enough calories to make space for today's lunch.

Sadly, today I did not have the luxury of collapsing into our massage chair and finding inner peace.

Instead, my agenda included checking on the battery status of the various phones, followed by a review of my plan to place the Tracker app on Marianna's phone.

By then, it was time for Marianna and Shahed to arrive.

Nysa and Siti had outdone themselves. The dining table groaned under the weight of multiple casseroles, tureens, bowls and platters, all of them filled to the brim.

At 12.30 p.m., we heard the familiar shout at the front door, 'Anyone home?'

Marianna came in and hugged and kissed Nysa, and then me. She looked beautiful, even though she was dressed in an old tank top and a floppy skirt that had seen cleaner days.

'So sorry, we were cleaning out our storeroom, and I lost count of the time! I barely had time to wash up before Shahed dragged me out!'

Shahed followed her, carrying a casserole and a cloth bag. As usual, he was dressed a little more formally than Marianna, in chinos and a polo shirt. Shahed was about five nine, and slim. His face had a pleasing symmetry but was unlikely to launch any ships.

'Hah! She woke up only at 10 a.m., Mom,' he chuckled, 'Don't listen to her excuses.'

Marianna punched him on his arm.

'Who made the Haloumi salad? Who made the cookies and brownies?' Marianna asked. 'And who was binge-watching Netflix while I was sweating over the stove?'

Nysa took the casserole from Shahed.

'Be nice to your wife, Shahed,' she said, 'she has access to your food.' She glanced at me to ensure that I got the message.

I took the bag of goodies from Shahed and walked them into the living room.

'What will you guys have to drink?' I asked, knowing their usual responses.

'I'll have a glass of that rosé you opened last week, Ishmael,' said Marianna. 'Do you still have some?'

'Of course, I have hidden it away from Nysa especially for you,' I replied.

'And I'll have a cold beer, Dad,' said Shahed, 'Watching Netflix is thirsty work!'

While I got their drinks, I was observing Marianna carefully. Not so much to look for signs of debauchery but to see where she kept her phone.

As she took the wine glass and sat down, she pulled out her phone from her pocket and placed it on the armoire in the living room. I looked at it carefully so that I could recognise it and not confuse it with Shahed's phone.

I glanced at Shahed—his phone was in his front pocket, and it stayed there.

'So, how was your week?' asked Nysa, sipping her weekly glass of red wine.

'I was in Phnom Penh this week,' said Shahed. 'What an amazing place. Every time I return there, I see distinct progress—new roads, new hotels and office buildings, more cars …'

'Yes, our firm is getting more and more business from Cambodia,' said Marianna, 'though a lot of it is from Chinese companies, rather than Cambodian ones.'

As we spoke, I scanned their faces and demeanours. Was their relationship in danger? Were the first signs of estrangement visible? It seemed not. Marianna was sitting close to Shahed, her left hand resting on his thigh. Shahed glanced at her a lot, smiling cheerfully.

I nodded and hummed and hawed, trying to keep my face free of the vortex inside me.

Nysa clapped her hands.

'Time for lunch!' she announced. 'I hope you are hungry. We have made your favourite dishes!'

'Nysa, when I know that we are coming over to your place, I make sure I don't eat breakfast,' laughed Marianna, as she rose. 'This is the highlight of my week!'

I rose and kept my glass on the armoire, next to Marianna's phone. I hadn't finished my drink. I pulled out the bottle of rosé and another can of beer from the wine cooler and took them into the dining room.

We sat down for lunch. Today, Siti had abandoned her Indonesian heritage and taken the Mediterranean route—lentil soup, pita and hummus, tzatziki, falafel, couscous salad and tahini sauce. We stood around the table feasting our eyes. Then, with due reverence, we served ourselves and dug in.

A few minutes later, I pretended to look around the table for my glass.

'Oh, I left my drink in the living room,' I said, ' excuse me.'

I rose from the table and went to the living room. Marianna and Shahed were oohing and aahing over each new taste. I picked my glass and pushed Marianna's phone off the armoire. It landed with a sharp crack on the marble floor. To prevent any ambiguity in its demise, I stepped on it hard and heard the screen crack.

'What was that, Ishmael?' called Nysa.

'Oh no, I knocked over Marianna's phone! It seems to have cracked,' I called back. As I kept my glass back on the armoire and bent to pick up the phone, Marianna came racing in.

'Oh my God!' she exclaimed. 'How did this happen?'

'I am so sorry,' I said looking as contrite as I could, 'I picked up my glass and brushed against the phone and it fell. So sorry …'

Marianna was checking to see if her phone worked. The screen was starred and quite opaque in parts.

'Oh, what do I do? I need to take a couple of calls later today,' she wailed.

Shahed came into the living room, carrying his plate. He looked at the phone and then at me reproachfully.

I straightened as if an idea just struck me.

'Oh, wait,' I said excitedly, 'I have a spare phone. Let me give it to you and I will get this repaired at the Apple store by tomorrow.'

I scuttled to my little hidey-hole and pulled out the new iPhone. I came back to the living room and handed it to Marianna.

'Why don't you transfer your SIM card to this phone, and check if it works?' I asked.

Shahed put his plate down, took both the phones and fiddled with them. He was quite a technical whiz. Within a minute, he powered up the new iPhone and passed it to Marianna.

'Just register a password, sweetie,' he said, 'and then sync your iCloud. I think you should be able to access everything you need.'

'Thank you so much, Shahed,' I said, 'and I am so sorry, Marianna. Let me take your phone and get it sorted out for you.'

'It's okay, Dad,' said Shahed, 'I'll do it, don't worry.'

That was not okay at all.

'No, I insist,' I insisted, 'my fault, and my responsibility. You guys have enough and more to do, I will get this repaired and bring it over to your place by tomorrow.'

Marianna's fingers were playing a concerto on her new phone. The screen flashed and dimmed multiple times.

A few minutes passed with Marianna focussing on the phone with me and Shahed looking anxiously on. Finally, she visibly brightened.

'Yes, my contacts are in here, and I am downloading WhatsApp and Insta. Thanks, Shahed.'

She continued uploading or downloading or syncing— whatever one does to transfer one's data from one phone to another.

I took Marianna's phone to my study and kept it on my desk. Then I returned to the living room.

'Come on, let's get back to lunch,' I said. 'So sorry to have caused you this problem.'

Shahed put his arm around Marianna and picked up his plate. They walked to the dining room. Marianna slipped the new phone into her pocket, probably to prevent me from wrecking it again.

'No worries, Ishmael,' she said, cheerfully, 'I am happy that I will be getting a new screen.' She smiled at me, clearing the air between us.

We rejoined Nysa, who gave me a dark look that said, 'Klutz!'

I smiled sheepishly and shrugged. 'So sorry for having disturbed everyone's lunch,' I apologised again.

We resumed eating.

The first stage of the first phase of my plan was complete.

CHAPTER 9

After lunch, we moved to the living room and collapsed on the sofas.

Our conversation was drowsy and sporadic.

I asked everyone if they wanted tea or coffee. No one did.

It was nearly 3 p.m. when Shahed and Marianna showed signs of rousing from their post-prandial stupor.

'It's time to go home, sweetie,' said Shahed, 'we are meeting the Lims for drinks at 6 p.m.'

'Yes, but I really want to sleep,' Marianna said, stretching like a satiated cat.

'You can catch an hour and a half at home,' Shahed offered, 'if we leave now.'

'Whose car have you come in?' I asked casually.

'Oh, Marianna's,' said Shahed. 'She thinks my Prius is beneath her dignity.'

'Absolutely, honey,' laughed Marianna, 'your goodie-goodie car will get eaten by my Audi R8!'

Taking a deep breath, I went to my study again and pocketed one of the Oppo phones. I also picked up my wallet.

By the time Marianna and Nysa had bid their eighteenth goodbyes, it was 3.30 p.m. As we neared the front door, I said, 'Could you drop me off at the petrol station? I need to get some cigarettes.'

'But you already have cigarettes on your shelf,' said Marianna. (Why did everyone keep track of my cigarettes?)

'Yes, and I also need some personal items,' I said, acting coy.

Marianna and Shahed exchanged a look.

'Sure, come on,'

Four minutes later, I was alighting from Marianna's car (she was right, this car could have had a Prius for breakfast), waving goodbye.

As they drove away, I felt a lightness of being. The Oppo phone was tucked deep inside a crevice in the car's rear seat, silent, yet so forthcoming.

I went into the Cheers store, purchased some cigarettes (though there were enough on my shelf) and walked back home.

As I did, I checked the Tracker app for both the iPhone and the Oppo. I could see Marianna and Shahed (and the car) entering their condo.

I shut off my phone and took the stairs up to our apartment. Nysa's lunches were magnificent, but they needed to be offset if I wanted to remain my svelte self.

Then, I took a well-deserved nap.

At 5 p.m., I took Marianna's phone and walked to Sim Lim Towers. I knew a small hole-in-the-wall service centre there whose owner knew more about iPhones than Tim Cook.

'Can you repair this, Darren?' I asked, holding out the damaged phone.

Darren took it and examined it from various angles.

'Looks like someone stepped on this,' he said, looking up at me.

'Yes, a silly accident,' I said ruefully.

'The phone seems to be okay,' he said, 'I can replace the screen. You want original or …'

'Oh, original, absolutely,' I said.

He quoted a price that only rocked me back a little.

'By when?' I asked. 'Tomorrow can?'

'Ummm, okay, tomorrow lunch time okay?' he asked.

'Yes, sure,' I said, relieved that I could keep my promise to Marianna.

'I will need the pass code to open and check,' he said.

I explained to him that this was not my phone but my daughter-in-law's.

'I will ask her for the pass code and send it to you,' I promised.

As I walked back, I opened my phone to check Tracker.

The iPhone seemed to be at 142, Kheam Hock Road. That must be the Lims, I thought. The Oppo was still at Shahed's condo. So Marianna does get into the Prius on occasion, I smiled to myself.

Back at the apartment, I said a quick 'hi' to Nysa and went into the study.

I opened my laptop and clicked on the Tracker app. I entered the codes for both the iPhone and the Oppo. Two screens popped up, one showing Kheam Hock Road and the other showing Shahed's condo.

I clicked on the dashboard icon on the first screen. It displayed an infographic showing the location of the phone and the time it had spent there. It showed the phone at our condo, the travel time to the petrol station, the brief halt, the travel time to their condo, a slightly extended halt, the travel time to Kheam Hock Road, and its current time ticking at the location. I did the same with the second screen.

Excellent graphics—easy to understand and record.

I left the study and joined Nysa in our bedroom, where she was watching an episode of *The Crown*.

She paused.

'Hi, Ishmael,' she said, 'all okay with Marianna's phone?'

'Yes,' I replied, 'I took it to Darren. He said he would give it back, as good as new, by tomorrow noon.'

'Good,' she sighed. 'Do you want to watch something else?'

'Not at all,' I said, 'I thought I'd join you. So what's happening with the Windsors? Or is it the Tudors?'

'The Windsors, silly,' smiled Nysa, 'the Tudors died out in the seventeenth century.'

I sat in the massage chair, put it on and watched entitled members of the Royal Family snipe and snarl at one another.

When the episode ended, Nysa switched off the TV.

'That's all?' I asked.

'Yes, it's almost 8 p.m.,' she said, 'let's have dinner.'

'Dinner?' I protested, 'I am still full from lunch!'

'Just a light meal, Ishmael,' said Nysa, 'some pita, hummus and tzatziki, that's all.'

I followed her into the dining room.

As promised, dinner was light, followed by watermelon and grapes for dessert.

'I have to get back to my research now,' Nysa said as we were clearing up, 'I need to send a proposal by tomorrow morning.'

'Sure, no worries,' I said, 'go ahead; I, too, need to finish some pending stuff.'

We parted ways and I went back to the study.

I checked the Tracker screen on the laptop. I noticed that Marianna's phone was now at Dempsey Hill.

'Hi Shahed, how are things? What are you guys doing for dinner?' I WhatsApped.

'Hi, Dad. We're having Vietnamese at Dempsey,' he replied a few minutes later.

'Great, have fun!' I said.

'Shall do, good night, see you soon!'

'Good night! And once again, my apologies to Marianna.'

'All good, Dad, sleep well.'

Another piece of the puzzle clicked into place.

Now to track Marianna's comings and goings, and identify the anomalies.

A sense of anticipation curled in my stomach. If I were into cliches, I would have said, 'The game is afoot,' rubbing my palms together.

CHAPTER 10

On Sunday, Nysa and I went for a long walk in the Green Corridor. This is a former railway line that linked Singapore and Malaysia. Now it has become this amazing, green walking trail connecting Woodlands and Tanjong Pagar.

We came back tired but refreshed.

We met at the dining table after washing up.

Breakfast mostly consisted of leftovers from the previous day's lunch, tweaked a little to give it a false veneer of novelty.

I complimented her.

'Give me a clove of garlic, a pinch of oregano, a drop of olive oil,' she declaimed, 'and I can change the world.'

Archimedes she was not.

After clearing the breakfast dishes, I decamped into the study. Nysa had planned a call with an old friend from KL and she disappeared into her room.

I opened the laptop and fired up the Tracker app.

I saw that Marianna (and her car) had left home at 11 a.m. and reached Plaza Singapura at 11.14 a.m. I didn't know whether she was accompanied by Shahed or was alone.

When I left the apartment at noon, she was still at the mall.

I walked briskly to Sim Lim Towers, to Darren's shop. He was his usual taciturn self. He handed me Marianna's phone. It looked like new.

'Passcode?' he asked.

I sent Marianna a message asking for her pass code, so that Darren could check if everything was in order. Within two minutes, she sent me the pass code. I read it out to Darren.

For the next few minutes, Darren put the phone through its paces, till it lived up to his expectations. He then handed it to me. I paid him, thanked him profusely and left.

On the walk back, I stopped for a Milo in Serangoon Road, and loaded the Tracker app onto Marianna's phone.

I called Shahed and we agreed that I could drop by at around 4 p.m. to hand over Marianna's phone.

Before leaving Serangoon Road, I stopped at one of Nysa's favourite eating places and ordered some food to go. It's always fun to surprise Nysa.

By the time I reached our apartment, Nysa had already laid out lunch. She was in the kitchen humming in sync with the microwave.

'Ta da!' I exclaimed, keeping the brown paper bag on the kitchen island. She recognised it immediately.

'Oh, rava thosai!' she cried, 'thank you so much, Ishmael, I was just dreaming of one!'

I told Nysa that I had picked up Marianna's phone and would be dropping it off at 4 p.m.

'Good,' she nodded, as we left the dining room, 'come, let's have a nice siesta.'

I tried to sleep but couldn't, so I read as Nysa napped.

At 3.45 p.m., I picked up the car keys and Marianna's phone. Before leaving, I checked the Tracker app on Marianna's replacement phone and found that she had returned home at 2.30 p.m.

Within ten minutes, I reached their condo and was buzzed up.

Marianna opened the door.

'So sorry to disturb you on a Sunday,' I apologised, 'just wanted to hand over your phone as good as new.'

'Thank you, Ishmael,' she said, taking her phone and opening it. Then she looked up at me. 'How much do I owe you?'

'Oh, absolutely nothing' I protested, 'it's my fault and I need to pay.'

Shahed came into the foyer.

'Here, let me switch your SIM card back,' he said. He took the phone from Marianna and went inside. He came back a few minutes later with Marianna's phone and my iPhone.

'Here, Dad, please take this,' he said, 'thank you for sorting this out.'

'Not at all,' I said, 'I am off now. Have a wonderful evening!'

That night, Marianna left home at 6.30 p.m. and went to Robertson Quay. Her car stayed at home. Evidently, the Prius was not completely useless after all.

Using the art of WhatsApp, I found that she and Shahed had gone for dinner at a Mexican place at the riverwalk.

One by one, most of the puzzle pieces were falling in place.

Earlier, I had realised that I needed a place where I would not be disturbed or caught out.

My study at home has an open-door policy and often Nysa or Siti would stroll in and out. It occurred to me that it would not be politically astute to be found tracking Marianna's phone or overheard calling and tracing her movements.

So on Saturday I spoke to Rajesh, a close friend who owned and ran his own trading company.

'Rajesh, I have a new gig and I need a cubicle to work out of for a couple of weeks,' I had told him.

'Absolutely no problem, Ishmael! I have three vacant cabins in my offices, and you are free to use any of them for however long you want.'

Over dinner, I informed Nysa that I had a new consultancy assignment and would be spending a few hours each day at the client's premises.

'All the best, Ishmael!' she said as she kissed me. 'I hope you enjoy the job.'

That night, I slept the sleep of the disturbed.

In the coming days, I thought, as I struggled to find a comfortable spot on my side of the bed, I would learn more about Marianna and Greg. I would either find them blameless or unfaithful.

If Marianna was not having an affair (and James' allegations were mere gossip), my life would return to its usual vanilla-like state, as I hoped it would.

However, if Marianna were indeed having an affair, I would need to act. I would need to find a way to sunder them. How was I going to do that?

Even if I did, what after that? If Marianna's affair was a symptom of a deeper malaise in her relationship with Shahed, then what?

When Shahed was younger, I was a Dragon Dad, more involved and prescriptive than I should have been. As he grew into adulthood, he grew into a wonderful person, strong but not overbearing, steady but not boring. By the time he was in his twenties, I had stepped back to let him get on with his life. Consequently, I knew very little about his and Marianna's marriage. They seemed good together, they laughed and talked like a couple who genuinely took pleasure in each other, they made for good dinner and picnic companions.

Other than that, I knew nothing. Did they love and respect one another? Were they satisfying each other's needs? Were they getting everything from the relationship they wanted and aspired for?

This was one of the times I regretted my lack of sensitivity. I had no idea about the state of their relationship. Even if there were some cracks in the binding, I was blind to them.

As the night deepened, I tossed and turned to a conclusion that I was trying to avoid—I needed to speak to Nysa.

I realise that I haven't told you enough about Nysa.

She is more beautiful than you can imagine. Her eyes captivate, her smile beguiles, her voice mesmerises, her presence excites.

Nysa is a polymath. She is talented in so many areas that I am constantly operating under an inferiority complex.

I have no idea why Nysa returned my adolescent affections. She could have had any boy she wanted. When she said yes to my proposal, I felt like I had hit the jackpot.

Nysa has a job that you wouldn't normally come across. She researches for writers. For novelists, screenwriters, nonfiction writers, speechwriters and TV producers. She searches hundreds of data bases, accesses libraries across the world, has a wide network of experts and specialists in many fields globally.

Nysa's research has helped publish more than fifty books so far.

But, more than her beauty or talent, much more than all of this, Nysa is truly caring, accepting, forgiving, empathetic and cheerful, which makes her the reason for my everything.

I am quite an asshole. I am arrogant and moody and annoying and tone deaf. I hurt and offend. My life could have easily been one of failure and frustration.

Then I met Nysa and for some reason, in spite of everything, she liked and put up with me.

Since the day we got married, everything I achieved, everything I gained was because of her. She was my Pygmalion, my Henry Higgins. She softened my brittle edges, blurred the ugly lines, papered over the cracks, smoothened rough spots. Nysa created a path for my few strengths to shine, unfettered by the bushel of weaknesses they had to shine past.

I was reluctant to speak to Nysa because I had figured she had had enough. Thirty-five years of pottery with uncooperative, friable clay must have been draining. I had decided that once I retired, I would try my best to make her life as happy and serene as I could, I would stand between her and the senseless brickbats that life seems to hurl at random.

Whatever my intentions, they seemed to be for naught. I would need to speak to Nysa. But not right now.

Interlude 3 – Shahed, Disturbed

I am tired. Really tired.

I am travelling all the time, and for what? To sell insurance products to companies who have never even heard of key man insurance or product liability insurance, let alone understand them?

Look at me now, 7 a.m. on a Monday morning and I am in a plane, even before my wife wakes up.

Sometimes I just want to chuck all this and walk away.

What is wrong with me?

I never used to feel this way. I know I am lucky. I am the youngest sales manager in the company; I am being paid nearly double what most of my classmates are earning. And selling is fun. Especially putting together a proposal that brings all the customer's requirements together in one interlinked package. I know I do this better than anyone else.

Of course I am lucky. We live in the most beautiful city in the world. We live in District 9, the poshest part of town. Mom and Dad are just ten minutes away. Money has never been a problem.

But these last two months …

I think it's because I can sense a growing distance between Marianna and me. I can't stand to even think that.

She is the love of my life. My sweetheart. My best friend. My present and my future.

But something seems to have changed, especially over the last couple of months.

Whenever I call her at the office, she's out, much more often than she used to be. Even her secretary doesn't know where she is half the time.

But when I ask her, Marianna says, no, she was in office, just outside her cabin.

I know she is keeping something from me.

Two days ago, she was on her laptop at the dining table, and when I crossed to get some water, she shut it and waited for me to leave.

Previously we used to talk about so many subjects, all the time, but now she seems to be lost elsewhere most of the time.

Am I imagining things?

The problem is that I can't speak about this to anyone. I can't tell mom. She will not take it well. She loves Marianna almost as much as she does me. She will find a way to raise this with her and I don't want that. Which husband wants his wife to feel that he goes running to his mummy every time he feels insecure?

And Dad? Dad will listen, analyse and draft a solution. But all of Dad's solutions involve confrontation. Have a frank talk, he'll advise. If your relationship is as deep and strong as you say, you should be able to communicate openly, he'll tell me. Logical, but of absolutely no use.

I wish I had at least one sibling. It would have been good to have someone to talk to, someone to unburden myself with. Ever since our marriage, I have gradually distanced myself from most of my close friends. I can't call them out of the blue and cry on their shoulder.

The question I am afraid to ask is, is Marianna losing interest in me? Is she seeing someone else, someone in her league?

I can't bear to ask this question. Or find the answer.

But I will have to.

As Dad says, however irritatingly, every truth is a part of your past, but every lie awaits you in the future.

I will have to figure something out. Once this damned plane lands.

CHAPTER 11

On Monday morning I rose earlier than usual and finished my run just as the sun gilded the streets.

I completed my ablutions and breakfast and left for Rajesh's office at 9.30 a.m. Rajesh was travelling but he had connected me with Linda, his assistant. I reached the office and was greeted by her, then shown to the cabin allocated to me. Linda gave me the Wi-Fi password, showed me where the coffee and cookies were and asked me to let her know if I needed anything.

I connected my laptop, my phone and the new iPhone to their chargers and opened the Tracker screens and dashboards.

On the laptop, I also opened an Excel file and quickly formatted it to list the stops and times. While I appreciate dashboards, I am a big fan of lists. They make me feel useful and they help me suss out patterns that I may miss otherwise.

I then took out my iPad, opened *The Economist* and settled to patiently wait and watch.

Monday passed slowly.

I finished reading *The Economist*, watched three TED Talks, downloaded the latest Baldacci novel and made significant inroads.

Marianna and her car arrived and stayed in her office building.

At 5.30 p.m., I called it a day. I was retired, unused to spending so much time in an office cubicle. I packed my stuff and returned home.

Nysa greeted me, as always, with a smile and a kiss and asked about my day.

'Boring,' I said, truthfully.

'I have made your favourite custard,' she said, and the day improved substantially.

'Thank you, sweetie,' I said, 'I am going for a quick walk, and will come back and dive into the custard!'

As I walked to the Botanical Gardens and back, the thoughts that had plagued my sleep last night kept pace with me. What if? What then? Why that? Why not?

Back home, I joined Nysa for dinner where my custard awaited. Custard is one of my comfort foods. It is smooth, silky and sweet, which is how I believe life should be. We watched two *Jeopardy* reruns and got about forty percent of the responses right.

At about 8.30 p.m., I went to the study and checked the phones.

Marianna and her Audi had left the office and headed straight for their condo, where both were now.

I texted Marianna. 'Hi M, hope the phone is working fine?'

'All good, thanks, Ishmael,' came the prompt response.

'Dinner done?' I asked.

'Yes, watching *The Crown*', she texted.

'Have fun, good night.'

'You too!'

I slept better that night. Sitting at a desk and doing nothing really takes it out of you.

Tuesday was a repeat of Monday, except that Marianna went for lunch to a food court next to her office. She was there for 38 minutes and spent the rest of the afternoon in her office building. Her car didn't move, till 7.30 p.m., when both of them left for their condo.

That evening, I engaged with Shahed. He was still in town but leaving the next morning for Ho Chi Minh City. We chatted desultorily, and I wished him a fun trip. I wished he wasn't going; the data so far suggested that whilst he was in town, Marianna's days were well structured and innocent.

On Wednesday, reality shifted.

At 11.45 a.m., Marianna and her car left the office building. By 12.05 p.m., they were in a boutique hotel on Joo Chiat Road. Hoping to find a simple explanation, I Googled the hotel to check if they had a restaurant that was known for business lunches. Then I called them. The hotel did not have a restaurant. Or even a bar.

I checked if there were any reputed restaurants nearby, where clients could be using the hotel parking lot. This is Singapore, and there were quite a few restaurants nearby, but none of note.

I called the hotel again. I used Rajesh's office landline.

'Good afternoon, would you have any rooms available?' I asked, when I was connected to the front desk.

'Yes, for how long would you need a room, sir?' asked the pretty voice.

Before I could respond, she continued, 'You can rent a room for 6 hours, 12 hours or a night.'

My heart sank. It was one of *those* hotels.

'Oh, thank you,' I said, 'let me come back to you. Have a good day.'

'And you, sir,' was the cheerful response.

For the next 70 minutes, I kept tracking the two phones, as if I was a deer caught in the headlights, seeing disaster hurtling, but unable to move.

At 1.40 p.m., Marianna and her car left the hotel. At 2 p.m., they entered her office building.

I sat back in my chair, feeling drained and weary.

Why was I doing this? Why did I think this was my problem to solve?

The rest of the day passed like maple syrup through a sieve. I couldn't focus on reading, the one TED Talk I tried to watch failed to drown the voices in my head.

At 4.30 p.m., I packed up and went home.

As I entered, Nysa came to me, smiling. As soon as she saw my face, her smile faded.

'What happened, Ishmael?' she asked, taking my free hand.

I realised that I was visibly carrying my woes.

'Oh nothing, darling,' I said, as soothingly as possible, 'some silly boardroom drama that was really annoying.'

Nysa was smarter than that. She was also smart enough not to question me. She looked into my eyes.

'Oh. Come, let me get you some fresh juice, and if you are up to it, let's go for a nice long walk.'

'That would be nice,' I said, grateful that she wasn't asking any more questions. 'Let me change and I will be with you in a moment.'

Nysa and I drove to the river, parked and started walking towards Marina Bay.

'Do you want to tell me about your day?' she asked, softly.

By then I had constructed a plausible alternate reality.

'Well, the four promoters and the two nominee directors got into a verbal brawl regarding cost trends,' I said. 'I tried intervening, but couldn't, wasn't allowed. After 15-30 minutes of this, I got up and said that I was leaving and would be back tomorrow to continue our discussion if they were willing to do so rationally. I am not sure if this assignment will continue or not ...'

Nysa listened carefully, nodding.

'And that's all?' she asked.

'Yes, it's annoying that I have to put up with such childish antics from senior professionals,' I said, getting deeper into character.

'Yes, that can be very annoying,' she agreed.

I glanced at her. Was there more to what she said than the words themselves?

'Sorry for being such a whiner,' I said, taking her hand.

'You rarely whine, Ishmael,' said Nysa, looking at me. 'That is one of the things I love about you. You solve every problem or try your best to. I am just concerned that there is more to this situation than what you are telling me.'

That last bit was Nysa's way of calling me a liar. She is a truly gentle person, other than when she is calling me an asshole.

I didn't know how to respond, so I kept quiet. We walked along the river, sparkling with reflected light, winding its way towards the sea.

When we reached home, we had a rather silent dinner.

Nysa went into the kitchen, and I hurried into the study.

I opened the phones. Marianna and her car had stayed in the office building till 8 p.m., and then reached their condo by 8.35 p.m.

'Hi, M,' I texted.

'Hey Ishmael.'

'How was your day?'

'Same old,' she wrote back.

'Any interesting cases? Grand larceny? Embezzlement?'

'No, one meeting after the other, that's all.'

'What did you do for lunch?' I asked.

'Ah, ordered a salad and had it at my desk. Boooring!'

'Want to come over for dinner tomorrow?'

'Would love to, but let me check my calendar? Revert tomorrow?' she texted.

'Sure. Have a good night!'

'You too, and Nysa!'

Did I tell you that I had a temper? I think I did earlier in the narrative. If I didn't, I'm sorry.

I have a temper.

It is a volcanic rage that rises from somewhere within my torso and burns its way up through my lungs and oesophagus and throat. When this happens, contrarily, I turn cold and deliberate and vicious. The world slows down, and my eyesight seems to gain clarity. I prepare myself to fight, but not brawl—to ruthlessly go for the jugular.

Many things cause me ire. Being lied to blatantly is one of them.

It took me more than half an hour to regain my normal composure. Only when I was sure that I was calm did I leave the study (after putting away the phones) to sit with Nysa on the couch, to watch Jack Reacher dismantle his opponents effortlessly.

CHAPTER 12

When I woke up on Thursday morning, I could feel the onset of a headache.

I hadn't slept well, and my body immediately protests any change in routine quite vociferously.

Also, my mood from yesterday had not yet dissipated. Crawling back under the covers became all the more appealing.

But I dragged myself out of bed, leaving Nysa deep in sleep, and went into the bathroom. My eyes were red and angry, and my face looked even more crumpled than usual.

As I brushed my teeth, I reviewed my plans for the day.

While jogging down Orchard Road and turning towards the Botanical Gardens, I reviewed my plans for the day.

As I prepared to leave for Rajesh's office, I reviewed my plans for the day.

My plans for the day consisted of, 'I have no idea what to do now.'

All my life, I have prided myself on getting things done. (Or, in today's parlance, I am humbled and honoured by my ability to get things done and am grateful for the support and blessings of my well-wishers.) I am rarely the smartest person in any room, however sparsely populated the room is, but I am usually the one who can take what is known and create a plan to move forward.

This time around, I was stymied. What do I do? If Marianna was betraying her husband and marriage for a sleazy affair in a skeezy hotel, what could I do?

I reached Rajesh's office at 9.50 a.m. and laid out my laptop and phones. I could see myself moving listlessly, wishing I was anywhere but doing this.

The anger from the previous day lay coiled in my diaphragm, a tamped down fire oozing smoke and sparks that were corroding my insides.

I opened the Excel file and the Tracker app and began checking the phones.

Marianna and her car were already at the office building.

There they stayed till lunchtime, when I left the cabin and walked over to the food court in the shopping mall two streets away.

A bowl of amazing Laksa followed by a large portion of Tau Suan eased my angst a little. I have never been able to figure out how these food courts sold amazing dishes for such incredibly low prices. And the food was better than most fine dining restaurants which charged five times the amount.

I walked back in a slightly better frame of mind and resumed my detection.

The day passed with no movement.

At around 3 p.m. I received a message from Marianna on the family WhatsApp group that she would not be able to make it for dinner tonight but would see us over the weekend. Nysa responded. I didn't.

At 5.30 p.m., I packed my stuff and drove back home.

That evening, Nysa and I took a walk along the Kallang River. It was a full moon, and atypically cool.

'How did it go today?' asked Nysa.

'Uh, what?' I asked.

'The story you told me yesterday about the argument between the promoters. How did that progress?'

Even after nearly four decades with Nysa, I am never sure whether she uses her words deliberately or whether I impale myself on the fabrications I erect.

I quickly gathered my thoughts.

'Oh, much better today. There was a lot of apologising and regretting and back-slapping. Each of them personally spoke to me and said sorry that they behaved the way they did. After that, things moved quite quickly.'

'So, you still have a job?' she asked.

'Yes, yes. We discussed a framework that would help reorganise the company around its two main revenue streams, and that seemed to align everyone.'

'That's nice. You seemed quite angry and upset yesterday. Much more than I would have thought you would be with a couple of silly promoters.' Nysa glanced at me as she spoke.

'What can I say, I am growing old and grumpy,' I joked.

'Yes, you are growing old. However, you have always been grumpy,' she shot back.

We continued walking in the moonlight, holding hands.

I rose early on Friday morning.

My weighing scale informed me that I should be sitting less at desks staring at phones and that food court Laksa portions were way too large.

I trust my weighing scale. It has no vested interest. So, I left home earlier than usual and jogged down Bukit Timah Road all the way to Sixth Avenue and then ran up towards Holland Road. My return trip was slower and more painful, but I was sure that my scale would be pleased with me. I sometimes feel that I live for its approval.

At 9.45 a.m., I was at the cabin in Rajesh's office.

Marianna and her car were safely ensconced in her office building.

I settled down at the desk and flipped open my iPad to the latest issue of *The Economist*. The cover announced that the world was going to the dogs. That was not unusual. *The Economist* is a dismal magazine, prone to weltschmerz. However, their articles were well word-smithed and their world views were grudging. I always felt better about my life after wading in their pessimism.

At 11.45 a.m., Tracker started showing signs of movement.

I kept my iPad down and opened the Excel file.

At noon, they were again at Joo Chiat Road.

I ground my teeth in anger.

I couldn't sit any longer, I started pacing. This was more difficult than it sounds. The cabin was all of 8 x 6 feet, and the desk was quite large. I opened the door and went into the common corridor. The building was in a light industrial park with long corridors that were mostly empty of people. I walked to the opposite end and returned. I paused and did it again.

I came back to my cabin and sat at the desk.

I wished I could reach out through the app and …

Wait.

I could go to Joo Chiat Road. I could verify whether Marianna and Greg were there together. Why should I sit here and speculate?

I bundled up my stuff and ran down to the parking lot.

At 1.05 p.m. I drove past Hotel Wellcome. I grimaced at the name. Obvious much?

It took me 10 minutes to find parking, almost half a kilometre away. I walked back to the hotel. Diagonally opposite was a small juice bar. I stepped in and ordered a fresh pressed juice, collected it and sat at a table next to the window. I pulled out my iPad and positioned it upright on the table and opened a book. I angled it so that I could look up from the iPad and see the entrance to the hotel.

One orange-carrot-kale juice and one pineapple-celery juice later (both drawn out as much as possible without making the Aunty suspicious) I saw Marianna coming out of the hotel. She was looking over her shoulder and speaking to someone.

Greg Closier stepped into view. They stood outside and spoke for a couple of minutes. He then stepped forward, kissed her on the cheek. She smiled at him lovingly and they parted ways, he went left and she turned right. A minute later, a car drew up beside Greg and he got in. It drove away.

A movement caught my eye. The hotel reception doors slid open again. Two men in suits stepped out. They were deep in conversation. They turned right and walked towards the hotel parking lot.

I continued sitting in the juice bar.

I opened the Tracker app and saw Marianna and her car pull away. Just as I was reaching for the phone to put it away, I noticed her moving away from the city, towards the airport.

I paused, Why was she …? Oh, Shahed was returning from Ho Chi Minh City today. Marianna was probably going to pick him up from the airport.

The violent rage returned in waves.

How could she! How could she go and meet her husband as if everything were normal just minutes after she betrayed him? Did she have a conscience at all? Was she completely amoral?

'Okay aah?'

I was startled. I looked up. The Aunty was standing next to my table, looking concerned.

'So sorry,' I said, standing up. 'So sorry. May I have the bill, please?'

She looked as if she was going to say something. Then she turned, made her way to the cash counter and printed out the bill. I gathered my stuff, paid the bill and left the bar.

At 3.30 p.m., I was back at Rajesh's office. I had no memory of how I had got there. I sat down heavily and stared at nothing.

Why us? Why Shahed? He is just a sweet boy. This will destroy him. Marianna was his life.

CHAPTER 13

That afternoon, I did not go directly home.

I could not.

I was still seething. There was no way Nysa would not notice that something was seriously wrong.

I drove to Plaza Singapura and parked.

I walked into the mall, took the elevator down and stepped outside. The day was grey and heavy, promising sheets of rain.

I turned left and walked towards Bras Basah.

As I crossed Queen's Road, a car shrieked to a stop. I looked at it and looked down. I was on the pedestrian crossing.

I turned to the car.

'What the fuck is wrong with you, you asshole!' I shouted.

I stepped towards the car and slammed my hands on the bonnet.

'Why the hell can't you see where you are going, you moron!'

The driver was a middle-aged man of Chinese origin. He waved at me, either in apology or in dismissal.

'Who the fuck do you think you are!' I shouted again.

His hand stuttered and fell to the wheel.

'You kiasu son of a whore!'

Suddenly, I realised that it was very quiet. Other than my shouting.

I looked around. On either pavement stood small groups of people staring at me wide-eyed.

'Watch where you are going, you stupid jerk!' I said, still loudly, but less than a shout.

I turned and walked past three youngsters who looked like students. They stepped back to let me pass.

I continued walking past NTUC, past SMU, past the Carlton. I had no idea where I was going.

The first drops of rain fell. Within 50 metres, it became a deluge. In seconds, my clothes were soaked and I was sploshing in water-logged shoes. I continued walking. The rain felt cool on my face and body, gradually ebbing away the frustration and anger, rage and sorrow that had taken over my being.

Rain is such a life-giving force.

I got back home by 8 p.m. By then, I had dried a bit, my clothes were damp but not soaking wet.

As I stepped into the house, Nysa called out from the dining room.

'Is that you, Ishmael?'

'Yes, sweetheart,' I called back.

'Thank God! I was getting worried. Why are you so late?'

'Let me wash and change and I will tell you about my day,' I said, walking past the dining room to our bedroom.

Fifteen minutes later, we were at the dining table. I was really hungry. Cold-pressed juices sound wonderful but they do very little for your calorie intake.

By now, I had my story down pat. I told Nysa about the brainstorming session we had, the new insights we discovered and how we couldn't tear ourselves away from the engaging task of conceptualising a new strategy that shattered traditional paradigms.

My objective was to bore her into somnolence.

I believe I succeeded. While Nysa tried her best to listen actively to what I was saying, I noticed her eyes glazing over two-three times. Each time, she shook her head slightly continuing to pay attention.

'That's nice,' she said weakly when I was done.

'Yes,' I said with enthusiasm, 'we are going to blue sky a new trajectory for the business, and quickly blitz-scale!'

'How wonderful,' she murmured, unable to muster any more interest or enthusiasm.

Feeling sorry for her, I asked, 'How was your day, darling?'

'Oh wonderful,' she said, perking up. 'I completed my research and went for a mani-pedi and a massage, and then Shahed and Marianna called from the car, and we spoke for a long time!'

She saw my face shift.

'What's the matter, Ishmael?' she asked, the familiar worry line appearing on her brow.

'Oh nothing,' I said, 'Was Shahed to come back today?'

'Yes, Marianna picked him up at the airport,' she said. 'Such a sweet girl she is!'

I speared a piece of watermelon and thrust it into my mouth.

'Ummff,' I grunted.

'Sometimes I don't even know why I tell you things!' Nysa huffed as she stood up and took her plate into the kitchen.

I took the opportunity and quickly decamped to the study. I closed and locked the door. I sat at my desk. I pulled out my notebook and looked at what I had written.

Step 1:
To confirm the allegations:
1. *How can I confirm the allegations without doubt?*
2. *What resources do I have at my disposal?*
3. *What tactics best fit this situation?*

I picked up my pen.

Below the three points, I wrote 'DONE'.

(I badly wanted to write, 'She's a lying whore!', but refrained.)

I continued.

Step 2:
To separate Marianna and Greg.
1. *How do I find out everything about Greg?*
2. *Where and how do I accost/confront him?*
3. *What approach would ensure a permanent separation between him and Marianna?*

I looked at the three bullet points for a few minutes. Then I kept my pen down and opened my laptop.

I started with LinkedIn.

By the time I joined Nysa in bed, I knew Greg better than many of his colleagues did.

He was British, born with a silver spoon and a safety net. He was 38, and a managing partner in an international law firm, which meant he was smart, ambitious and ruthless.

Greg was married. His wife was Jocelyn Wong, a partner with Ernst & Young, a global consultancy.

Jocelyn Wong belonged to the Taipei Wongs, Taiwan's largest real estate family. So Greg was not only rich, he had married richer.

He played golf. He was a member of the Island Club and the Tangerine Club.

Greg and Jocelyn partied and entertained a lot. They liked to post pictures of themselves, their drinks, their food and their friends for others to see and envy.

Greg liked to gamble. He was a very welcome guest at the MBS casino. He also flew to Macau regularly.

Greg drove two cars—a Lamborghini and a Porsche.

He and Jocelyn lived in a Black & White on Cluny Road.

They did not have children.

He fucked other men's wives.

Greg Closier seemed to have the life that most people aspired for but never achieved.

All this was good to know. But it was not enough.

Segue 2 – Ishmael's Notebook

— November:

Task 1:

~~To confirm the allegations:~~
   ~~1. How can I confirm the allegations?~~
   ~~2. What resources do I have at my disposal?~~
   ~~3. What tactics best fit this situation?~~
DONE.

Task 2:

To separate Marianna and Greg.
   1. How do I find out everything about Greg?
   2. Where and how do I accost/confront him?
   3. What approach would ensure a permanent separation between him and Marianna?
Follow on notes:
   1. Info on Greg?
      a. Social media?
      b. Mining—dark browser?

    c. *Tracker?*
    d. *Others?*

2. *Where and when?*
    a. *Office?*
    b. *Clubs?*
    c. *Restaurants?*

3. *Approach?*
    a. *TBD*

CHAPTER 14

'Shahed and Marianna are coming for lunch,' said Nysa when we were having breakfast on Saturday morning.

I looked up. I had just returned after playing two hours of tennis and was famished. I was slurping up yoghurt with little heed for decorum.

I did not want to see Marianna. I could not risk seeing Marianna, with the anger that was still roiling inside me.

'Oh, I have a lunch meeting today,' I said, falling back on the easy lies I had perfected while working, to avoid things like performance appraisals and audit meetings.

'You never mentioned a lunch meeting,' said Nysa, 'if you had told me, I would have asked them to come over for dinner.'

'It just came up last night, dearest,' I mollified. 'Not to worry, what time are they coming? I will spend some time with them and then leave.'

'You always do this,' she muttered, quite unfairly, I think. I do this a few times, but not always.

'I am so sorry, Nysa,' I said, 'but this is a new assignment, and I am feeling my way through the first couple of weeks.'

I was milking my 'consultancy assignment' for all I could.

I felt quite comfortable with my lying. After all, I was doing it for the sake of harmony. It was not safe for me to sit in the same room as Marianna and not show the disgust, anger and loathing I felt.

As we cleared up, Nysa cleared her throat. I looked up.

'What are your plans for tomorrow?' asked Nysa.

'Why?' I asked.

'No, just tell me if you have any meetings or lunches,' she said.

'No, nothing for now,' I said, cautiously.

'Good,' she said as she walked into the kitchen.

I looked after her for a moment, then continued clearing up. Who was I to even attempt to understand what went on in her mind?

As I was washing the breakfast bowls and plates, my mind returned, as it had done numerous times over the past day, to Shahed.

Shahed was a wonderful young man. I know that I am probably biased given that he is our son, but I tend to be reasonably objective about such evaluations, regardless of relationship.

Shahed was smart and capable. He was also generous and kind. What irked me and had always annoyed me was that he was also naïve and gullible. He trusted most people, he took things at face value, and he wouldn't recognise a political move if it hit him in the face.

Shahed worked with an insurance company, United World Insurance, as a sales manager. He was their youngest manager, a position and achievement that he had earned. He was one of their biggest rain-makers. He travelled a lot on work.

Shahed had inherited some of his mother's talents. He was an amazing chef. He painted like a maestro. He loved cars and knew them better than their manufacturers.

Shahed was a good son. He never went through a rebellious phase, like most teenagers do. He was liked by almost everyone who knew him, and many who didn't.

I understood the concept of Karma, of 'what you sow, so shall you reap'. This was even more reason why I couldn't come to terms with the fact that Marianna was cuckolding Shahed.

What had he ever done to deserve this? He had never caused any harm, by action or inaction. He always stood up to be counted. He always gave more than he received.

Why is this happening to him?

I always thought that Marianna was his greatest blessing. Now, it looked like she was going to be his nemesis.

I swore to myself that I was going to do whatever it took to protect him from deceit and disillusion.

By 9.45 a.m., the kitchen was spotless, I was in the study, ready to continue my research.

Years ago, when I was in marketing and sales, we hired a young computer whizz kid. I was forty-two years old then. He was exactly half my age. Any computer came to life under his fingertips and yielded all its secrets to him without hesitation. We spent only about eighteen months together before he left for greener pastures. He is in his late thirties now and has a personal net worth of five hundred million dollars.

Despite our age difference and the generation gap, we hit it off quite well. He would come over to my cabin frequently and pepper me with questions on business models and revenue streams. I liked his enthusiasm and curiosity.

Seeing his command over this new and exciting domain made me realise that I was a dinosaur. Information Technology was the future and I needed to know how to navigate it, if not master it.

One afternoon, I spoke to him.

'Hari,' I said, 'I want you to teach me as much as I can learn about computers and IT. I am happy to pay you for your time and skill. Let me know what you think is appropriate.'

He didn't pause for a second.

'Ishmael, my pleasure,' he said, 'but I don't want money. I want you to help me build a couple of business cases for ideas that I have in mind. And I want you to help me find an investment partner from amongst your network.'

I didn't hesitate either.

'Done,' I said.

We shook hands on it.

Over three months, he taught me how to mine the internet. Not just surf, not just search, but to dig deep and extract. Not everything he taught me was strictly legal. He gave me a toolkit that I could use to pry open different parts of the internet and peer inside.

I was a willing student. I had long realised that information is power, and the more you have of it, the less vulnerable you are. And the prospect of having information about the market, about our customers, that my competitors did not have? Priceless!

In the years after his tutorials, I leveraged my learnings efficiently.

Customers were always pleasantly surprised, sometimes even a little spooked by my intimate knowledge of their innermost strategies and plans. They gladly gave me their business once they heard how my offer neatly dovetailed with their aspirations.

Vendors were not so pleasantly surprised when I trotted out accurate figures of the mark ups that they were charging us. They had no choice but to revise their offers. Our competitors would have been furious had they known how much cheaper our purchase prices were than theirs.

Competitors often wondered how we bid just a little lower and just a little better than them, time and again. How much time they must have wasted investigating if any of their own people were leaking sensitive information!

I am not going to describe the tools that he gave me. There's no point. If you don't know what they are, it'll be impossible for me to explain them to you. If you know what they are, you don't need me to explain.

I hadn't used the toolkit in a while, since I had retired, and it took me a few tries to scrape the rust off. Then, like before, the virtual world opened its doors and passageways to me.

When I arose from my chair at 11.30 a.m., I knew Greg better than most of his close friends.

Greg was operated on for a slipped disc when he was twenty-eight years old.

He was allergic to peanuts and shellfish.

He preferred Italian and Mediterranean food.

He dated at least three women before he met and married Jocelyn.

He made more than two million Sing Dollars a year.

He owned two houses in England and three properties in Singapore.

He liked to run, and he liked dogs. He donated generously to SPCA and ACRES.

He had received many awards from various forums, each of them extolling his capability as a lawyer.

He fucked other men's wives.

If it hadn't been for the last, I believe I would have quite liked Greg Closier. He seemed to be a stand-up person, a self-made and successful professional.

As I rose, I recalled the last time I had done such a deep-dive was just before I retired. The Board of Metrocyn had hired an international executive search firm to find candidates that they could interview for the post of CEO. There were already two internal candidates but the Board was right to expand the search.

The Chairman had called me.

'I think we've found a great candidate, Ishmael,' he said, 'I am sending you the CV, could you please review it and give me your views? I think this is the one.'

The candidate, an American, currently working with a competitor, looked amazing. Great education, solid experience, an enviable track record. He offered glowing testimonials from past employers. I was just about to reply to the Chairman with my blessing. But something nagged at me. The CV seemed too perfect. I strive for perfection, but I distrust it. Perfection is not natural.

So, instead of sending an email, I closed the door to my office, told my secretary to ensure that I was not disturbed for an hour and went down the rabbit hole.

It took me fifteen minutes to find that he had been fired from two companies in the United States for fraudulent behaviour. However, as is the norm in that country, he had hired lawyers and taken them to court. As part of the legal settlement, he remained fired, but bound them in confidentiality clauses that meant that they could never inform anyone about his misdeeds.

I found a former colleague of his who had now retired and didn't give a damn about the confidentiality agreement. I wrote to him and he wrote back, narrating the full account of the candidate's misdeeds.

When I left Metrocyn, I was glad that I prevented the company from falling into the hands of an unscrupulous, conniving bastard. I handed it over to the safe hands of my deputy, Dexter, whose job was to ensure that the company grew in leaps and bounds.

I left the study and went looking for Nysa.

She was in our bedroom, in the massage chair, multitasking. She was getting a massage, drinking tea and reading on her iPad.

I was surprised.

Normally before the kids came, Nysa would be scuttling around making sure everything was enough, perfect, more than enough. She seemed rather relaxed today.

'Hi, sweetheart,' I said, sinking into the settee next to the massage chair. 'When are Shahed and Marianna coming?'

Nysa did not raise her eyes from the iPad.

'Not today,' she said, 'I've rescheduled the lunch to tomorrow.'

'Oh?'

'Yes, today you can have your business lunch without any guilt,' she said, 'what time will you be leaving?'

'Oh?'

Nysa glanced at me.

'Ah, I should be leaving any time now,' I said, rising from the settee, 'thank you for postponing the lunch on my account.'

She smiled at me sweetly and returned to the book she was reading.

I left the bedroom. Where should I go for lunch, I wondered. I decided on the Ion Orchard food court. I picked up my wallet, phone and iPad and put on my walking shoes.

Interlude 4 – Nysa, Agitated

I was right.

Something is going on with Ishmael.

He is involved in something serious. And he is trying to hide it, I know. But he can't hide anything from me. It sounds cliched but I can read him like a book.

He is lying to me. To me, his wife of thirty-five plus years! And not once or twice, multiple times. Making up fairy tales. What does he think, I was born yesterday? All that bullshit about new assignments and promoters having fights—he has forgotten that I read the same books and watch the same movies as he does!

And he is definitely avoiding the children.

I cannot, for the life of me, understand the last part.

Ishmael dotes over Shahed and Marianna. He always loves meeting them, enjoys talking and joking with them, and is always ready to go out of his way to help them if they need anything at all.

Ever since Shahed brought Marianna home the first time, Ishmael adopted her as his daughter. I remember Ishmael helping her prepare for the interview with Nestor

& Ross, patiently pulling together dozens of probable questions and helping her draft the best responses. I remember his delight when she called and screamed that she had got the job.

What is going on?

Has either of them offended him or hurt him in some way?

I don't think so. If that were the case, Ishmael would have confided in me. He knows that I can mediate such issues.

There is something more, something bigger.

I am really worried. Ishmael seems like a harmless, middle-aged man, but he has a ruthless streak in him. He doesn't see the world as most of us do. He is very Biblical—an eye for an eye and a tooth for a tooth kind of person. Once someone gets on his wrong side, he can be quite unforgiving.

I still remember the day I first saw Ishmael. It was at Far East Plaza. They had just announced the opening of their computerised musical fountain. There was such a rush—everyone wanted to see this novelty! We were not there for the fountain, of course; my friends and I used to hang out at Far East regularly. I remember sitting for hours at Ya Kun Kaya and having coffee, chatting.

Dobrina and I were about to leave after spending most of the afternoon shopping and eating. That's when I saw Ishmael. Through the glass, so to speak. He was right outside the mall, holding the door open for an old woman with a walker. She was moving quite slowly and a crowd was gradually building behind her. Suddenly, a really rude man tried to push past her. I saw Ishmael lift his left arm and hit the man on his nose with his elbow, without actually seeming to do anything. The man fell back, clutching his face. It was so funny. And then, Ishmael, while still guiding the old lady in, apologised profusely to the man for 'his mistake'. Then, Ishmael made sure he let everyone else in before he allowed the man inside. Almost as if he was punishing him for his rudeness.

Dobrina wanted to leave, I remember. She was getting late for something. But I stood there and watched Ishmael walk in finally. He was alone. It looked like he was surrounded by a bubble that kept him separated from everything else. He looked around at everything but didn't approach, touch or buy anything.

I don't know why but I felt sad for him. I didn't even know him at that time, but I felt from the bottom of my heart that someone needed to break that bubble, hold this man and take care of him.

When I told Dobrina this, she looked at me like I was crazy.

'He's not even that good looking, Nysa,' I remember her saying.

'I know,' I had replied, 'but he needs someone to talk to, to share his fears with, to confide in,' while I watched Ishmael turn the corner and disappear.

Dobrina laughed at me. After a moment, I laughed at myself, too. What was I thinking?

It's been almost forty years since that day now.

I still feel Ishmael needs me to take care of him. I don't want him to be doing something that will get him into trouble. He is not impulsive or accident-prone, I know. I also know that he plans and thinks through everything he does, but still. He is still macho and self-righteous and thinks he can fix everything.

What frustrates me is that I don't know why he is not confiding in me. He always talks to me about everything. What is different this time?

I think he is in pain and ready to lash out.

And I don't know how to protect him.

CHAPTER 15

When I returned from my lunch and walk, I went to the bedroom. The curtains were drawn and Nysa was taking a nap.

I slipped out of the bedroom and went into my study.

I pulled out my notebook and looked at my list.

I knew everything (or nearly everything) one could reasonably know about Greg without using protection. I knew where he lived, where he worked, where he played, and sadly, where he screwed.

The next two questions I needed to answer were:

One, where and when should I confront him?

Two, what did I need to do to separate him and Marianna?

I opened my laptop and pulled up all the files on Greg that I had saved.

I opened the Excel file that I had used to track Marianna and pulled up a new worksheet.

I spent the next four hours laboriously plotting as many of Greg's movements as I could, extracting information from various postings on social media.

He usually played golf at the Island Club on Wednesday and Saturday mornings.

He ran in the late evening, but not routinely.

He and Jocelyn went out at least twice a week to various high-profile restaurants, but rarely by themselves. Most of the time, they were in groups of eight to twelve people.

They had two helpers, one Indonesian and one Filipina. They also had a gardener who came thrice a week. They did not have a security guard.

Greg travelled two or three times a month. Short trips—to India, Thailand or Malaysia. He only travelled SQ first class. There was no discernible pattern in the frequency or duration of his visits.

At 6.30 p.m. I sat back, exhausted.

I closed the open documents, the Excel file, my notebook and the laptop.

I got up and opened the door to the study.

'Is that you, Ishmael?' asked Nysa from the kitchen.

'Yes, Nysa,' I answered, the dutiful husband.

'You had your door closed, and I didn't want to disturb you,' she said, as she came to the head of the staircase. 'Are you finished for the day?'

'I am finished for the month, I think,' I told her wryly.

'Would you be a darling and pour some wine for both of us? I have made some curry puffs and tapioca chips, it would be nice to chill out a little.'

'That sounds like heaven, sweetheart,' I responded enthusiastically, 'I will do it right away. Just give me five minutes to wash my face and you will be served.'

'Thank you, my unsung hero,' she said, turning to return to the kitchen.

We had a lovely evening, both of us had more wine than we were used to. We spoke faster and laughed louder than our ages prescribed. Siti had prepared a wonderful dinner as always, and I ate too much. I looked at the time, wondering if I could do a quick walk, but both my watch and my body indicated otherwise.

Also, Nysa was giving me come hither looks. Either that or she was developing astigmatism. So, we went to bed, and I discovered that her eyes were perfectly fine.

I slept the sleep of the exhausted and the replete.

We woke up to a lovely Sunday morning. The sky was grey and overcast, and a cool breeze played with our curtains.

I came out of the bathroom after brushing my teeth and washing my face.

'I am going for a run, Nysa,' I announced.

She stirred, opened her eyes, and smiled at me.

'Good morning, sweetie,' she said.

'Good morning! And sorry I woke you up,' I said, leaning over and kissing her.

'Mmmm. No, you go ahead and run, I am going back to sleep,' she murmured.

'Bye, darling.'

I put on my running clothes, shoes and stepped out of the building lobby. A light rain had begun falling.

I loved running in the rain.

Running by itself is such a clarifying experience. It drives out all the cobwebs and uncertainties and ambiguities that accumulate in my brain. Running in the rain is even better. It is like a high-pressure wash. Every time I complete a run in the rain, I feel renewed and rejuvenated. At least for a short period of time. Then, of course, my sixty-year body reminds me of my age.

I returned home to the aroma of thosais and sambar. I would have loved to dive in, but I was sopping wet, and Nysa would not have been amused if I dripped puddles of water across her beloved parquet floor.

After I had towelled myself and changed into clothes that did not squish, both of us were enjoying steaming portions of crisp thosai smothered in chutney and sambar.

'Don't forget, the children are coming for lunch today.'

I looked up. I had forgotten. This is what wine and women do to a man—they make him forget.

'Oh?'

'And you don't have any meetings or appointments or calls today?' Nysa stated.

'Ah?'

'So, please see if our stocks of wine and beer are sufficient,' she continued, ignoring my monosyllabic, rather moronic responses, 'and please shave, you are thirty years past the era when a stubble looked sexy.'

'Mm-hmm,' I responded.

While it would not be fair to say that the thosais had turned into ashes in my mouth, it was true that my enjoyment of the breakfast had diminished substantially.

As we were clearing the table, and I was completing the washing up, I wondered how I was going to deal with that afternoon. Much as I would like to think that I am stoic and inscrutable, I am not. I wear my heart on my sleeve and my emotions on my face. It was going to be near impossible to sit across Marianna and smile. Both Nysa and Shahed knew me well and would spot that something was wrong.

As always, when faced with a problem, I retreated to my study.

I sat at the desk and pulled out my notebook and fired up the laptop. No point wasting time, I thought, I need to figure out an approach to deal with Greg.

As I could see it, I had four options to confront him:

One, at his home.

Two, at his office.

Three, at the Island Club, his golf club.

Four, at one of the three restaurants he and Jocelyn seemed to frequent regularly.

None were ideal.

Greg and Jocelyn had helpers coming out of their ears at home. Not to mention gardeners and pest control engineers and random guests.

His office, as I said, was all glass and glare. Any discussion would be visible to the entire firm. Unless we met in the restroom.

At the golf club, Greg would surely be part of a foursome. Buttoning him privately would raise eyebrows and handicaps.

The restaurants themselves were not great, but here again, the restrooms were a more viable option.

Actually, there was a number five on the list.

The car parks at his office and club and the parking lots at the restaurants.

If you watch Netflix and have a penchant for thrillers, you will see that most unsuspecting people are accosted in car parks. They are also beaten, ambushed, strangled, shot, knifed and poisoned in car parks and parking lots. According to Hollywood, more people died in car parks every year than they did in the two World Wars.

I understand why.

From what I had observed, car parks are, as a rule, gloomy and isolated. There are lots of nooks one can hide in. People don't linger. They are either focused on getting to the elevator or finding their car. Also, the elevator or stairwell is usually at least half a kilometre from wherever their car is parked. This gives any miscreant enough time and opportunity to plan, prepare and execute their nefarious deeds.

In Singapore, car parks don't have the same reputation that they have in the US. It has been ages since anyone was molested, mauled or murdered in a Singapore parking lot. This has led to a sense of false security among Singaporeans. They enter car parks without a care, never looking over their shoulders or peering carefully into their cars before getting in.

This may be an opportunity.

I took out my notebook and wrote down my ruminations in terse bullet points.

Then, I prepared to meet Marianna.

CHAPTER 16

Living with Nysa has been very challenging for me. Mainly for my waistline.

Even before we got married, Nysa was an amazing cook. Since then, she has expanded her repertoire and mastered many more cuisines—Thai, Chinese, Lebanese, Italian, Indian. She fuses them together in amazing and innovative ways.

Directly as a consequence of her expertise, for much of my life, I was heavier than I should have been. I was what you would call a well-rounded person. About two years ago, I had an unpleasant encounter with a full-length mirror in a hotel bathroom. I did not like what I saw. I decided that I would do something about it.

The next day I started running.

I stopped after 100 metres.

I could not continue. I was wheezing and gasping and panting. Pain shot through my chest, lungs, knees and feet. I really thought that it was time to meet my maker.

When I recovered, I did what I always do when seeking to surmount a problem. I looked for an expert. I spoke to Darren Liao, the fittest person I knew.

'Darren,' I said, 'I need to lose weight. I feel and look like a walrus. I need your advice.'

'Ishmael,' he replied, kindly, 'at your age, don't do it alone. Even with the best intentions, you could hurt yourself. I suggest you find someone who can guide you and ensure that you achieve your goals without blowing out your knees or throwing out your back.'

'I agree,' I said, though a hint of resentment coloured my voice. I was not *that* old. 'Anyone you would recommend? For someone of my advanced years?' I couldn't resist that last sentence.

Darren groaned.

'Come on, Ishmael,' he said, his voice long suffering, 'you know I didn't mean it that way. But, yes, I know of one company. They are new on the scene but are delivering amazing results. They are called Athleaders. It is run by a young German chap. Truly professional. Ninety percent plus success rate.'

'Oh, excellent,' I responded with enthusiasm, 'could you connect me to them?'

'Of course,' he said, 'I will do this today. I will ask Bernhard to call you ASAP.'

That was the beginning of the end; of the layer of fat that covered me.

Bernhard and I spoke. Then we met. He took me through some paces. He asked me what I liked and what I did not. And then he devised a program for me.

Over the next few days, I discovered I could walk reasonably long distances. Without stressing my ankles or knees. So I did. In time, during my walks, Bernhard suggested that I jog short distances, which became slightly longer, and even longer. Every week, Athleaders reviewed my progress, tweaked my program, and cheered me on.

Within six months, I could see my toes. After a year, I could even see my penis without the help of a mirror.

Now, I am svelte. And lissome. And sylph-like.

When I started walking and then running, I also cut down on my eating. It was not easy. When you live with Nysa, you are prey to the aromas wafting from her stove and from her oven, it takes every ounce of willpower not to drool.

In the beginning, my abstinence annoyed Nysa. She claimed that I had fallen out of love with her. It took a lot of convincing to get her to understand that I wanted to get into shape and would love her regardless of my form.

And regardless of her form.

Nysa, unlike me, is not sylph-like. Or if she is, it must be one of the more prosperous sylphs. Nysa likes carbs, sweets and munchies. She believes that if God had meant humans to run, He would have given them wings.

But she loves me. So now, at the dining table, we mostly eat fruit and salads, yoghurt and sprouts (yes, I agree with your 'ugh'). When we are not eating these, Nysa snacks on chips and biscuits. She hoards them by her bedside drawer.

When the children come home, however, Nysa throws caution to the winds.

Today, the dining table was a riot of taste and aroma and colour. There were salads, rice and roti-prata. Laksa and pasta, kebabs and curries. There were cookies, brownies, cupcakes and parfaits. There were poppadoms and chips.

There was enough food for our entire condo.

At 12.30 p.m., we heard the familiar voices. Shahed and Marianna had arrived.

I steeled myself.

I thought of pleasant things—of *Bambi* and Rocky Road ice cream; of running in the rain and *The Big Bang Theory*. I channelled my inner peace. Then, I went to the front door.

Marianna was hugging Nysa. Shahed saw me and smiled.

'Hi Dad!' he said and hugged me. I hugged him back, tighter than usual.

'Whoo!' he said, 'you've still got it, old man!'

I punched him lightly on his arm.

Marianna turned to me.

'Hi, Ishmael,' she smiled, 'you look slimmer every time I see you!'

She stepped forward and hugged me, as she always did when we met.

For the first time, I did not hug back.

My arms refused to move from my sides. I gritted my teeth and lifted my right arm and patted her on her back.

She stepped back with a slight frown.

I smiled.

'So nice to see you both!' I said cheerily. 'Come, come, let's have a drink before the scrumptious lunch Mom has made!'

The moment passed.

We had our ritual wine and beer and chatted about Singapore's weather ('How hot it is nowadays!') and politics ('What do you think of this year's budget?') and traffic ('Where are all these cars coming from?').

I did my best to lean forward, smile and meet everyone's eyes. I poured drinks and offered snacks.

'Are you travelling again this week?' Nysa asked Shahed.

'Yes, mom,' he replied, 'Three days in KL.'

'Oh, I love KL,' said Nysa. 'Can I come with you? Your father never takes me anywhere!'

'Shahed doesn't take me either,' complained Marianna, half-joking.

Shahed looked at her. He had an unusual expression on his face.

'I have asked you many times to come with me,' he said, mildly, 'but you are always too busy, Anna.'

Marianna had the grace to look abashed.

'Yes, that is true, dearest,' she said, 'the last couple of years have been hectic beyond words.'

'But,' she continued, 'soon, I should have more time and then I will be able to come with you and see all the exotic cities you travel to!'

'You are very lucky, Shahed,' said Nysa. 'One week in Ho Chi Minh City, another in Jakarta, a third in Phnom Penh. It would be amazing just visiting all the different restaurants and markets in each place.'

'Mom,' Shahed protested, 'your idea of a trip is very different from mine. I spend most of the day trying to convince people to buy insurance. This means I am stuck in offices and meeting rooms, not gallivanting around sampling different cuisines!'

'How boring!' exclaimed Nysa.

'When I was travelling,' I chipped in, 'initially your mother never appreciated the fact that each trip was onerous and had agendas that started at 8 a.m. and finished at 9 p.m. Only later, when she accompanied me on a few of those business trips, did she realise how busy and packed they were.'

'True,' said Nysa, 'but I had a wonderful time, lolling around in five-star hotels and getting massages and pedicures and shopping in those quaint little flea markets. I wish I could have done more such trips.'

'It was always fun travelling with you, Nysa,' I said, looking at her, 'but I felt guilty that we couldn't spend more time together exploring ...'

On that note, we adjourned for lunch.

Both Marianna and Shahed are quite slim. But they can put food away like industrial vacuum cleaners. Just before the dessert course, there was a moment when I wondered if there would be enough food for everyone.

Shahed pushed away his plate finally.

'I am stuffed!' he said. No wonder. He had polished off more than I could eat in a week.

'So am I,' said Marianna, 'Nysa, each weekend is a more delightful experience than the previous one! We are so lucky!'

Then why are you screwing around with Greg, I wanted to say but did not. To offset my thoughts showing on my face, I smiled and nodded. It took a lot of effort.

As he rose from the table, Shahed turned to me.

'Dad, would you like to take a walk?'

I looked at him. This was unusual. Normally, Shahed would move the thirty steps from the dining room to the living room and collapse on the sofa.

'Sure,' I said. I turned to Marianna and Nysa and asked, 'What about you two?'

'Oh no,' said Marianna, 'I am going to sit next to my mother-in-law and watch TV.'

'I could not have asked for a better daughter-in-law,' said Nysa, laughing.

Shahed and I levered ourselves off the chairs and helped carry the dishes into the kitchen and load the dishwasher.

We then waddled to the front door, put on our shoes and made our way to the elevator.

We walked out of the condo grounds and turned right towards Orchard Road.

CHAPTER 17

I loved Shahed more than life itself.

As I have said earlier, he is a wonderful son. An all-round wonderful person, actually.

I know this sounds like a fond father's bias. But Shahed is a genuinely good person. I worry about him a lot. He is nice but naïve, intelligent but innocent. I would do anything to protect him from the senseless disappointments that the world inflicts.

Most of my acquaintances from the corporate world would be shocked to hear such sentiments coming from me.

'Ishmael said that?' they would scoff. 'Ishmael Dollah, the same guy who fired the entire management team of Borgian Holdings within a week of his taking over the company? Are you kidding?'

Or.

'Don't be ridiculous!' they would exclaim, 'you are talking about a cold, calculating bastard who has Freon running in his veins. There is no way Ishmael has ever felt even the slightest of emotions.'

They would not be far wrong. I always focus on getting the job done. Anything that stands in the way is collateral damage.

If there are too many people for a company's revenue stream to support, then most of those people have to go. That is the only way forward—what is there to discuss?

If a management team has allowed a company to slip into distress and illiquidity, they don't deserve to be in the company any more. They had their chance and they blew it—there are no extenuating circumstances to ponder or consider.

Being willing and able to take tough, unemotional decisions is what made me the darling of private equity and business magazines.

But Shahed, Shahed is different. He is my son. It is my duty to protect him, to ensure he is not harmed. To stand between him and the world's myriad cruelties. To do whatever it takes to keep him safe and happy.

'So, how are things, Shahed?' I asked, not allowing my thoughts to colour my voice as we entered the throngs of helpers and shoppers crowding the pavements even though the sun was blazing down.

He took some time to respond. I put it down to the amount of effort his digestive system must be putting in.

'Well, mostly okay,' he said.

This was very un-Shahed-like. He is usually positive and gung-ho about life.

Alarm bells began to ring.

'Mm-hmm,' I said, noncommittally, dodging a family of four carrying forty shopping bags.

'Work is fine,' he continued, 'the travel is a bit painful but I am learning a lot, and will need this experience if I am to take on a regional role soon ...'

'Mm-hmm.'

'I just got a couple of new guys on my team and inducting them is taking quite a bit of my time,' he said, 'so I am coming home later and later, even when I am in Singapore.'

'It must be tiring,' I said.

'Not very tiring, but ...' he responded, 'but, I am not spending much time at home, and Marianna ...'

'Mm-hmm?'

'Well, Marianna ...'

'Mm-hmm?'

'She must be feeling lonely, no?' he asked, almost as if he was talking to himself.

'Maybe,' I responded, 'but she also has her work which keeps her quite engaged and busy, so it seems like a two-way street to me.'

'That's true,' he nodded, 'both of us are on fast tracks, and that requires us to put in long hours every day, and even sacrifice weekends and holidays. But she doesn't travel so much, and I am travelling all the time.'

'Yes, Shahed,' I said ruefully, 'every dream, every ambition has its price, its flipside. There is no escaping that.'

'As far as I am aware, the only viable approach is for both of you to align your expectations of one another,' I continued, 'and keep communicating openly and continuously.'

Shahed nodded.

'Have you spoken to Marianna?' I asked, 'have you discussed the impact that your jobs may be having on your lives?'

'No,' he said, looking at the pavement, 'but then, we really haven't been speaking very much these past few weeks.'

Then, he turned to me.

'How did you and Mom manage?' he asked. 'I know you travelled a lot on work. Did Mom resent that? Especially because she was largely a stay-at-home spouse?'

I thought for a while.

'You will have to ask Mom,' I said, 'I never really thought of this. In our time, we recognised and accepted that we both had our parts to play and did our best to support each other.'

I paused and thought a little more.

'But you are right,' I said, 'Mom must have felt lonely, especially when I was travelling to the US and Brazil, for two weeks or more at a time. There were years, Shahed, when I used to travel more than 120 days in the year, practically an absentee husband and father.'

I considered it a little more.

How could I tell Shahed of the worries and fears that plagued me when I was away? Of being scared that Nysa would seek companionship with someone else to offset her loneliness? Of the dark thoughts that assailed me when I called home from a distant destination and the call was not answered. Of listening carefully to her voice for any cues that may reveal her happiness in my absence?

How could I tell him of this constant fear that I had carried through so many years, whilst hiding it behind a veneer of macho confidence?

How many contemporaries had I seen have their lives upended, marriages ruined, distanced from their children, hearts hollowed out?

I cleared my throat, and my head of these unpleasant memories.

'At least she had you,' I said, 'And you were enough to keep her busy from dawn to dusk!'

He chuckled.

'That is true,' he said, smiling at a memory I couldn't fathom. 'I have driven her crazy so many times. There must have been instances when she must have wanted to run away to escape the mayhem!'

His face softened.

'I know that I missed you a lot when I was growing up,' he said, almost sadly. 'I never understood why you were away so much. Sometimes, I thought that you didn't like me and that's why you stayed away …'

My heart ripped apart.

'Never, Shahed, absolutely never,' I said, my eyes moistening. 'How could you think that for even a moment? Every day I was away, I would be counting the days till I came back home and have you run into my arms!'

'I know, Dad, I know,' he said kindly, 'but this was when I was very young. As I grew older, I realised that you had to travel for work, and that you were delighted to come back to Mom and me.'

'You know, Shahed, I don't regret much,' I said, 'but the one thing I truly regret is losing a lot of your childhood.

Sadly, that was the time I was building my career, and I had to achieve certain milestones to make sure I progressed on my path to the corner office.'

'I understand, Dad,' he said.

Shahed may understand now, but the fact that I put Nysa and him through the absence of what should have been their anchor—was any corner office really worth the cost?

'I wonder if Marianna understands,' he added, softly.

I felt it was time to go beyond 'mm-hmm'.

'Is there a problem, son?' I asked.

Shahed was quiet for a few steps.

'Hmm, no, nothing really,' he said, 'just some minor issues. Don't worry about it, Dad, it will pass.'

We continued walking,

'Are you sure, son?' I tried one last time.

'Yes,' he said, glancing at me and giving me a reassuring smile, 'it's nothing.'

It was not 'nothing'. Shahed had definitely sensed that something was not quite right. As of now, it was limited to suspicion. But he would, sooner or later, act on it, and then he would find out the truth.

When that happened, it would be too late. Shahed was not a pussy-whipped pushover. If he discovered that Marianna was cheating on him, he would walk out and away. And that would be a disaster for him, and even an inconvenience for her.

I had to do something about Greg. And quickly. As lawyers loved to say, time was of the essence.

Interlude 5 – Jocelyn, Distraught

He is doing it again.

Greg is cheating on me. Again.

How can he do this? Especially after the last time when he knelt in front of me, cried and promised that he would never again break his vows. He swore on his parents, for God's sake.

This is the fourth time. Or the fifth. I don't even know any more.

What is wrong with me? What am I not able to give him? Why is he constantly looking for comfort elsewhere? I am beautiful. I know this, people have been telling me so since I was a child. Even Greg's friends say so, in front of him and when he is not around and they want to hit on me. I maintain myself. I spend more than fifteen hours a week at the gym. My personal trainer, Bernhard, tells me that I'm fit.

I am not dumb. I am up-to-date on any topic that Greg wants to discuss. Our house is always clean, elegant and welcoming. We dine on all the foods that he enjoys.

What is missing in me that he strays so easily, and so often? I never refuse sex; in fact, most of the time, I am the one initiating our love making and Greg is the one saying he is too tired. I host his friends and colleagues and bosses, and make sure that I help him build the networks that he needs to achieve his ambitions.

What am I doing wrong? I don't argue or whine. Am I being too submissive? Does he think of me as a pushover? As some kind of arm-candy? I don't ask for anything. Does that make him insecure? Should I show him that I am more dependent on him? Will that make him see me better?

First, at least the first one I know of, was the British Ambassador's wife. That bitch, Penny Mulliner. We weren't even married for two years then. I couldn't believe it. She was not even that good looking—a cheap, brazen whore with bright red lipstick and a laugh like a horse's neigh. Till today, I don't know what Greg saw in her. How much pleasure it gave Vera Oon when she made cow eyes at me and said how sad it made her to tell me what Greg was up to. I was so happy when her husband Marshal left her to run away with their Filipino maid. Served her right!

Then it was his secretary in his old law firm, Thelma. A stupid bimbo with a 38 D-cup. Is that all Greg wants? Huge breasts? Should I go for enhancement surgery? I am only a 32. Is that putting him off? I remember Greg coming back smelling of cheap perfume and cheaper champagne, and mumbling how much work he had and why he had to stay late in the office. Lying, cheating bastard.

Last time was the last straw. Greg was having an affair with a client's wife, for God's sake. What was wrong with him? He could have been disbarred and become the laughing stock of the legal world. This time, I didn't need Vera Oon to tell me; there was a line of people happy and willing to break the news. *I* became the laughing stock. How humiliating it was. I told Greg I was leaving him. He could go wallow in the mud for all I cared. And then he cried and apologised and promised and begged.

I shouldn't have agreed to stay. But the fact is that I love Greg. I have loved him since we first met at the National Gallery Gala. I love him so much that it breaks my heart each time he does this to me. Why can't he see that? Why can't he realise how much I love him and how everything I do is to make him happy?

I wish somebody could tell me what I am doing wrong. What is missing in me? At least then I can do something about it. Now, I have no idea. I am completely lost, unmoored, drifting in a sea of pain and hurt.

I need a drink. Let me pour myself some scotch. It will help dull the pain, for a few hours at least.

I feel so alone. I can't speak to ma-mah and baba— they will never understand. They have been married for forty-two years and have never looked at anyone else. All my so-called friends are only too eager to stand on the side lines and watch the next episode in this 'desperate housewife' saga.

The only person I can speak to is Aunt June. She is the only one who listens and understands. But she is so far away. And she's busy all the time, travelling across the world on work.

I'll finish my drink and call her. I'll ask her to tell me what is wrong with me. Why is Greg not finding what he wants in me? What can we do to make sure he never cheats again?

CHAPTER 18

On Monday morning, at 10 a.m., I reached Marianna's office building.

I had taken the MRT to Raffles Place.

I thought it would be better if our car wasn't registered in that parking lot. For the time being, at least.

I walked into the lobby.

The elevators to the car park levels were on the left. I took one and pressed B3.

I stepped out into a small foyer. On the right was a fire door to the main car park. I opened it and walked in and around the car park.

After about 15 minutes, I retraced my steps and left the building.

What was wrong with Singaporeans?

The car park I had just exited was nothing like any car park I had seen on Netflix or Amazon or Hulu.

It was bright, shiny and clean, with nary a nook or corners.

Cars stood socially distanced from one another, preventing the possibility of lurking unnoticed.

There were multiple entrances and exits, through which smiling, chattering groups of people poured through without pause.

And cameras! There were more cameras in that parking lot than there were in Universal Studios. I must have been photographed more than a hundred times. I was sure that somewhere, someone was peering into a multitude of screens and wondering why I was skulking around that parking lot and triggering the latest in facial recognition software to determine whether I had any pending Interpol notices.

Cancel car parks.

I stepped into the familiar confines of the Raffles Place MRT station and took the train back home.

After a quick stop, during which I picked up my stuff, I drove to Rajesh's office.

In my cabin, I looked through my contact list. I called two numbers and struck gold on the second. I had arranged an invitation for myself for a drink at the Island Club that evening.

That done, I opened my laptop and started looking at the three restaurants that Greg and Jocelyn liked.

Two were in large and expensive malls. Which meant that the car parks would be similar to the one I had visited earlier. Which meant that they were not of any use.

The third restaurant was in Dempsey Hill.

I have been to Dempsey Hill often. It used to be some sort of Army Barracks in the days of the British occupation. Now it has become home to some of the best restaurants in Singapore. The layout is colonial, with sprawling single-level buildings, surrounded by trees and knolls.

I knew that Dempsey Hill had an unorganised car park with parking lots squeezed in between the former barracks and spread out beyond them.

The Dempsey Hill parking lot had potential. It was closer to the Hollywood-kind than any other in Singapore.

I decided to first go to Dempsey Hill, spend a few minutes there, and then vend my way to the Island Club.

I still had some time before I had to leave for home.

I opened Google Earth and started looking at The Island Club and Dempsey Hill.

When I packed up, I had a reasonably good idea of what I was going to encounter that evening.

I reached home, kissed Nysa, and told her about my plans for the evening. Re-told, actually, as I had already messaged her.

'Will you be having dinner there or at home?' she asked.

'I should be back home for dinner, sweetheart,' I responded. 'If there is any change, I will let you know ASAP.'

'Okay, have fun,' she said, giving me a quick kiss before heading to the living room.

I went to the study and sat at my desk.

I pulled out my notebook and reviewed all the notes I had collated so far.

No new inspiration struck me.

I put it away.

For the next half hour, I went through everything I had so far.

The only next step was to find a place where I could meet Greg. If I couldn't find one, I would have to consider other options.

Should I find a way to lure him somewhere?

What would interest him?

I opened the laptop. I opened the various files on Greg that I had downloaded and re-read them.

Jocelyn and Greg collected art, I saw. More Jocelyn than Greg. Should I engineer an art sale? How? I had not the faintest understanding of art.

Greg liked high-end cars. Could I do anything with this?

They did not seem to have pets. A dog would have been useful. It would have to be walked sometimes, and that would have enabled a quiet meeting.

No solutions presented themselves.

I shut down the laptop and went to change up for my evening out.

'Bye, Nysa,' I said, as I was leaving.

'Bye, darling,' she replied, 'don't forget to let me know about dinner.'

'Shall do,' I said, kissing her on her head, and left the house.

It took almost thirty-five minutes to reach Dempsey Hill. The traffic was getting worse every day.

I parked near a Vietnamese restaurant. There were enough lots as it was still early in the evening. I walked around the three main blocks. The place looked quite promising. There were a few locations that were not as brightly lit. There were others that were a little remote.

Greg and Jocelyn frequented a well-known Greek restaurant. This was at the far end of the block. There weren't too many parking spots outside. However, a little further, on the right was a line of parking lots, dimly lit and about a hundred metres from any of the buildings. It looked like a good spot for a private meeting, I thought.

I took another round of the area, and fixed various points of interest in my head.

This was a useful recon.

I got into my car and drove to The Island Club on Island Road. It was a massive club, abutting MacRitchie Reservoir. An amazing place, really.

I met my friend Derek Francis at the main lobby. He was about my age, originally from Australia, living in Singapore for more than thirty years. His wife, Shu Ling was Singaporean, and a lovely person. She and Nysa were good friends.

'So good to see you, Ishmael,' he said, warmly. 'It's been ages since we caught up.'

'Absolutely, Derek,' I said, 'my fault, I have been out of circulation for a while.'

'Everything okay?' he asked, as we walked to the Island Bar.

'Oh yes,' I replied, 'I've just become lazy and housebound,' I laughed.

We sat at the bar. He ordered a scotch for himself and a rum and coke for me.

'Derek,' I asked, 'would you mind giving me a brief tour of the club after this? I am thinking of taking up golf, you see.'

'Hallelujah!' he cried, 'I have been trying to get you to do so for years! Of course, I will give you the VIP tour. What caused this change of mind?'

'Well, while working, I always felt that I wouldn't have enough time to allocate for golf,' I lied smoothly, 'now that I am retired, I thought, why not?'

'You have finally come to your senses, my friend!' he said enthusiastically. 'Let's take a look around, and if you need anyone to sponsor or second you, just let me know!'

Fifteen minutes later, we left the bar and started the tour. Derek had evidently done this before. He sounded like an expert docent. He took me into every hall, every corridor, every restaurant, every changing room and washroom.

Contrary to my original assessment, the club had a lot of potential. It was large and spread out. It was sparsely populated for the most part, with people congregating in a few oases. There were many rooms one could step into briefly if one wanted privacy.

On the way, Derek introduced me to a few of his friends. We also met a couple of mutual acquaintances. All of them encouraged me to take up golf, enthusiastically.

After about an hour, we returned to the bar.

'One more drink?' asked Derek. 'And, what do you think?'

'I think I am lucky to have you as a friend,' I said, warmly. 'Thank you so much for the wonderful tour. As for the drink, is it okay if I take a rain check? Nysa is waiting for me for dinner.'

'No worries,' he said, 'why don't you and Nysa join us for dinner next week? I know Shu Ling has been wanting to catch up for some time.'

'Of course!' I said, 'It'll be our pleasure.'

With that, we said our goodbyes and I went to my car. I stood next to it and reviewed what I had seen and learnt.

This is a good location for a meeting with Greg, I thought.

CHAPTER 19

On Tuesday morning, I decided that I did not need to go into Rajesh's office. I could work from home.

I woke up later than usual and went for a slightly longer run. Then I showered and joined Nysa for breakfast. I told her about my meeting with Derek, and his invitation for dinner.

'Yes,' she said, 'Shu Ling already messaged me. We are discussing dates. Is next Friday evening okay for you?'

After we worked out two dates that suited both of us, I told Nysa that I needed to work on my assignment and came into the study.

I sat down at my desk, opened my laptop, and started scanning the various social media platforms.

Normally, Jocelyn and Greg loved to post, not just about what they were doing or eating but also who they were meeting, and what they were planning to do and eat.

Their feeds were strangely silent this morning. There was the odd share and like from Jocelyn, but nothing from Greg.

I moved onto the internet.

I looked for any Dempsey Hill restaurant 'specials'—food tastings, wine pairings and so on. Again, everyone seemed to be fast asleep this week.

Then I visited The Island Club website to see if there were any tournaments or parties planned. Strike three.

Running out of options and things to do, I checked out the art scene. Ah. At least the artists were active. There were two single-artist showings and one multi-artist showing planned for Thursday and Friday. One of the galleries was in Dempsey Hill.

I called them.

'Good morning,' I said to the (presumably) young lady on the other end of the line. 'May I speak to your manager?'

'I am the manager, Sheila Duncan,' she said, courteously, 'how may I be of help?'

'Hi, Ms Duncan,' I said, 'I am calling from Nestor & Ross, the law firm. Our managing partner is an art connoisseur and has indicated interest in your showing on Thursday. I wondered how I may obtain an invitation for him?'

'Oh, it is my pleasure,' she replied. 'And what is the Managing Partner's name?'

'Greg Closier,' I said, 'he may already be on your list. He is on quite a few, I know.'

'Just give me a minute, please,' she requested. After a while, she spoke again.

'So sorry, Mr Closier is not on our list. But I will be happy to include him,' she said. 'Where may I send the invitation?'

I read out Nestor & Ross' address.

'I will despatch the invitation today. Thank you and I look forward to seeing Mr Closier on Thursday evening.'

'Thank you very much, Ms Duncan,' I said, 'have a lovely day.'

I ended the call. I spent a few minutes pottering at my desk. I rearranged the pen stand and sorted the pens and pencils by relative height.

Then, having nothing else to do, I went to the balcony off the living room and lit a cigarette.

What could I do to force a meeting with Greg? I thought, as I watched the cars slowing down as they entered the roundabout far below, their brake lights winking on and off.

Short of inviting him for a duel at dawn, I shook my head with a smile.

Should I look for a mutual acquaintance? One who could put us together? But the moment we are introduced, he would know that I am related to Marianna. She and I share our last name. And that would give rise to questions for which I had no answers.

The cigarette was down to its last breath. I stubbed it out in the ashtray on the table in the balcony.

I leaned on the railing and continued to search for options.

'Ishmael, are you ready for lunch?'

I was startled. I turned around and saw Nysa. She stood there smiling.

'Looking for a solution to another of the world's problems in the smoke, huh?' she asked. 'You are so predictable, you know.'

I smiled. I was glad that she thought I was predictable.

'Yes, I am hungry,' I said, 'what's for lunch?'

'Watermelon salad, dhal curry, yoghurt and spiced corn,' she said.

'Wow, that sounds amazing, let's go,' I said.

After lunch, I went back to my study, opened my laptop and checked Greg's social media feeds again. No luck.

I went into the browser and looked for Nestor & Ross' main landline number.

I took out the Oppo phone and called.

'Good afternoon, this is Nestor & Ross, how may I help you?'

'Good afternoon, this is Charles D'Souza calling from Windsor Marine,' I said, pulling two names out from my past. 'I was referred to your law firm and was asked to speak to one Mr Closier. My company has a large M&A deal coming up, and I was wondering …' I deliberately tapered off.

'Hello, Mr D'Souza,' said the nice young lady. 'Could you give me a few seconds to check if Mr Closier is available?'

'Of course,' I said, 'I'll wait.'

The strains of a symphony played in my ear.

'Mr D'Souza,' said the young lady, 'so sorry to keep you waiting. I believe Mr Closier is not in office; he is travelling. I checked with his secretary, and she suggested that I connect you to Ms Marianna Dollah, his associate?'

I almost dropped the phone.

'No, no,' I said. 'Not to worry, I will tell my boss that Mr Closier is out of town. Will he be in next week?'

I spent the next couple of minutes extricating myself from a very determined attempt to get my phone number, e-mail address and office address. I finally fell back on an old hack.

'I am so sorry, I have another call coming in, may I call you later?'

I dropped the phone on the desk. That was too risky. I should not do it again.

Five minutes later, the Oppo phone rang. It was Nestor & Ross. I switched off the phone and put it in the desk drawer.

Stupid!

I got up and walked out of the study. I couldn't afford to make such errors. I couldn't afford impatience.

At least, I told myself, I had obtained one piece of information.

Greg Closier was travelling. So, a meeting with him this week was unlikely.

I wandered a bit from room to room. Then I stepped into our bedroom. Nysa was on the couch, typing on her laptop. She looked up.

'Are you finished for the day, Ishmael?' she asked.

'Yes, mostly,' I said.

'Just give me a few minutes, I need to send a couple of e-mails,' she said.

I walked over to the massage chair and sat down. I fiddled with the controls and started a back and shoulders and foot massage. The chair started vibrating and kneading and pounding.

After a few minutes, Nysa closed her laptop and kept it beside her. She tucked her feet under her and looked at me.

'Sweetie, may I share something with you,' she asked, tentatively, as if she were unsure herself of what she wanted to say.

'Of course,' I replied. I switched off the massage.

'You need to keep this to yourself,' she said, as a preamble.

'Of course,' I repeated.

'Ah, I am not sure how to say this, but …' she stumbled, her face showing unusual distress.

'Go ahead,' I urged, leaning forward.

'I think Shahed and Marianna are having problems,' she burst out.

'Mm-hmm,' I said.

CHAPTER 20

The worry line was back on her forehead, deep and centre.

'I don't have any solid reasons, but something is not right ...' Nysa continued, her voice carrying the familiar undertone of misery whenever she is discussing any problem that the children may be facing.

'Shahed is not his normal cheerful self,' she said unhappily, 'and there is, there is a distance between them that wasn't there before. I don't know how to explain it.'

'Have you spoken to him?' I asked, 'or to Marianna?'

'Oh no,' she shot back, 'I can't interfere in their lives!'

I looked at her.

'If we are going to help, we will need to interfere, isn't it?' I said reasonably. 'We will need to know what is happening if we are to help find a solution.'

She considered what I said and nodded.

'Yes, but ...' she said, haltingly.

'What do you think is happening?' I asked, 'you have very good instincts. What are they saying?'

Nysa thought for a few seconds.

'It seems to me that Shahed is drifting away from Marianna for some reason,' she ventured, 'I don't think Marianna is aware. I don't know. Maybe Marianna is working too much and Shahed is feeling ignored? Maybe something is not right in their bedroom?'

Do you remember me telling you that I would need to speak to Nysa sooner or later?

It seemed the opportunity had finally come.

I leaned forward.

And then I saw the light shining off the tears in Nysa's eyes. Nysa doesn't cry easily. She is a strong person, our family's bedrock. In fact, the only times she has cried in our marriage is when I have been even more of an asshole than usual.

I got up and went to sit beside her. I held her hands.

'I just want them to be happy,' she said, her voice breaking just a little.

'I know, I know,' I said, squeezing her hands.

'What do we do?' she asked.

I didn't answer her. I sat there, holding her, knowing that I couldn't do anything this week.

What is the use of planning and preparing, I thought angrily, if external factors prevent progress? I had little control over Greg's movements.

I needed to expedite the meeting with Greg, I thought. If not this week, I will make sure it happens by next week. Come hell or high water.

'Do you think we should speak to Shahed?' asked Nysa.

I pondered her question.

'I am not sure, Nysa,' I said, 'what can we speak to him about? That we feel that there is a distance between them?'

'I am also wondering,' I continued, 'Are we overreacting? Don't all couples go through their ups and downs? Could this be just a temporary phase?'

'I hope so,' said Nysa, 'I hope it is a storm in a teacup. It seems more than that, though. I can't explain it, but ...'

As I said earlier, Nysa is a true empath. She can sense things most people can't.

I needed her to restrain herself for a few days, though.

'Why don't we do this,' I suggested, 'let's give it a week or two and see if the situation resets itself. If it doesn't, let us call them in and have a family discussion. What do you think?'

Nysa was silent for a few moments.

'Okay,' she said, 'that is a fair approach. In the meantime, I will keep speaking to both of them on and off. I'll keep my finger on the pulse.'

'Good idea,' I said, hiding my relief, 'and if either of them wants to confide about anything, they have the opportunity to do so with you.'

Nysa took a deep breath and got up.

'I have an important deadline coming up,' she said, 'and I have not been able to focus. Let me see what's happening with dinner, then I want to spend an hour or two and complete the first draft of the report.'

'Absolutely,' I said, rising with her, 'you go ahead. I also need to add the final touches to a document I am working on. See you at dinner.'

Nysa left for the kitchen and I moved to the study.

I sat in my chair and put my feet up on the settee, facing the bay window.

Yes, time was of the essence, but it was best not to push too hard either. If the choice is between doing it right and doing it fast, the former always wins. Hands down.

I had learnt that very expensive lesson in Axxon where one of our product lines was industrial chemicals.

An important customer in my stable wanted us to develop a substitute for a critical chemical that they were currently importing at an exorbitant cost. The customer used almost twenty tons each year. The opportunity was huge.

I sat with the technical and production teams. We discussed—first, whether we could do this. They evaluated the chemical's components and said yes. Then, we discussed how long it would take to reverse engineer the formulation, the lead time for the constituent chemicals and the production process. All told we agreed that we would need about ten weeks.

When I responded to the customer they were not impressed. They needed three tons within the next month, they said. They wanted us to prioritise this for them. They hinted at giving us 100 percent of the business.

That is when I made the mistake.

Dollar signs flashing in my eyes, I went back to the technical team and brought all the pressure I could to bear on them to speed up the development.

'Ishmael,' the technical manager said, 'it is not simply a matter of developing the formulation. Once that is done we need to test it on specific parameters. These tests take a week, sometimes two, and one even takes four weeks. If we try to bypass these tests, we are taking unnecessary risks.'

I didn't want to accept his warning.

'Come on, Ben,' I said, 'this is a once in a lifetime opportunity. Twenty tons a year, at a hundred and fifty dollars per kilogram—that's three million dollars! If we don't do this, they will go to our competitor. This business will vanish in a puff of smoke.'

I pleaded and persuaded and bullied and pulled rank.

I won.

And then we lost.

The three tons were delivered within thirty days, as promised. And the formulation failed on two parameters.

The customer was furious. I had personally let him down, their CEO said.

My boss was disappointed. That made it even worse.

The production and technical teams had worked night and day. They were devastated.

The worst part?

'Ishmael,' their CEO said, at a meeting a couple of months later, 'if you had told me about the extended testing beforehand, I would have imported the first three tons, and then switched over to you.'

That was the last time in my life that I put speed before quality.

I finally fixed the situation and the relationship. It took me almost four months and a lot of crawling and begging and self-flagellation. It was not something I was eager to repeat ever again.

Yes, it was frustrating that the Greg situation was pushed back because of things beyond my control. Yes, the sooner this was resolved, the better.

Yes, if an opportunity presented itself, I would grab it with everything I had.

But, if circumstances said, 'wait', I would heed their words.

Interlude 6 – Nysa, Hurting

First, it was Ishmael. Grumpy, hiding something, lying to me, trying to solve his problems all alone.

Now it is Marianna and Shahed.

Of all the couples I have known, Shahed and Marianna are the perfect, 'made-for-each-other' kind. Their love shines so obviously. They rarely argue or fight. They enjoy each other's company. They go out of their way to support one another.

What is happening? What is causing this distance between them?

It is all very well for Ishmael to say, 'Wait and see', but how can I? My children are in trouble and I am supposed to wait?

At least Ishmael is a grown man. Whatever problems he is dealing with, he has the experience and knowledge to find a solution.

Shahed and Marianna are children. They have been brought up in a cocoon. They received everything on a silver platter. They don't know what real trouble is!

I remember when, about four years ago, Marianna thought she was pregnant. What a tither she was in! 'Oh, we are not ready yet,' she said. As if anyone is ever ready for a baby. I remember her calling me a hundred times and dropping in twice a day. Luckily for her, it was a false alarm. How she broke down in tears in sheer relief!

And Shahed is no better. He was nearly thirty when he had that minor accident on Balmoral Road. And the first thing he did was call Ishmael and ask him to come over to the site. Later on when I asked him why he had called his father to deal with a minor problem, he went all sheepish and silent.

Will they be able to cope with a serious issue?

This situation sounds just like Yin Mei's daughter. Everything seemed fine till one day she came home and said that she had fallen in love with another man, and was leaving her husband. Yin Mei and Barun were shocked out of their wits! Even now, after almost two years, they have not been able to make peace with this. And poor Melvin, he didn't know what hit him—he looks completely lost every time we see him at the club.

I don't want anything like this to happen to Shahed and Marianna. Yes, they love each other and care for each other, but that is not enough!

Why don't people realise that marriage needs continuous attention and work? That it is a fragile plant that needs to be nurtured and nourished constantly?

A couple can't meet twice a week and once on a weekend and expect everything to go swimmingly. Shahed is travelling all the time. Marianna is in office till late night almost every day. When do they actually spend time together?

I don't like what Ishmael and I have agreed on. But since we have, I will wait for another week.

And why the hell doesn't Ishmael do something?

He is supposed to be this amazing CEO who goes into terrible situations and turns them around. His friends speak of him with awe—about how he rescued that company and how he transformed this company. Why can't he do the same with Shahed and Marianna? Why is he saying that we should wait? What does he expect will change suddenly?

Can't Ishmael sit them down and read them the riot act? I know how tough he can be—I have heard him on calls chewing people out. I remember feeling sorry for most of them. That's what these silly children need; someone to get them to wake up and smell the coffee. Someone to ram it into their heads that they must protect and nurture what they value.

I don't care. If things don't improve, I am going to sit both of them down and give them a straight talking to. If Ishmael wants to help, great. If not, I will handle it myself.

I am NOT going to allow what happened to Yin Mei to happen to us.

I am not going to allow a shadow to darken their lives.

One week. After that they have to deal with me.

CHAPTER 21

The rest of the week passed slowly.

I went to Rajesh's office on Wednesday and Friday, to keep up the narrative. I sat there and read *The Economist* and did crossword puzzles. On Thursday, I completed some long pending chores.

I did not track Marianna. Greg was travelling, and I doubted that she was that promiscuous that she would be conducting multiple liaisons.

On Wednesday night, Nysa and I went mall-hopping on Orchard Road, window shopping amongst various designer brands that amused both of us with their pretence. Why on earth, Nysa said, would anyone wear black, purple and green stripes, unless they were completely colour blind?

Shahed was in KL till Friday. Marianna had told Nysa that she was very busy this week. She promised to come over during the weekend once Shahed was back.

On Saturday, I went for my run in the morning. On the way back, I stopped at Fennel and bought breakfast for Nysa. She loves their thosais. I got her a masala thosai with extra portions of chutney. She scarfed it up. I gave her company with my yoghurt and fruit.

Before lunch, I quickly scanned Greg's and Jocelyn's social media to check if any restaurant visits were planned. No. Jocelyn had put up some pictures of herself with some friends at the opening of a new upscale gym. No sign of Greg.

After lunch, Nysa and I lay down and watched an old Bond movie. *GoldenEye*. Nysa loved Pierce Brosnan. We both loved James.

At 4.30 p.m., I rose, kissed Nysa and prepared for my tennis game.

Most weekends, I play tennis at the club. Sometimes early in the morning, and others in the later afternoon. We have a regular foursome, and our games are a highlight of my week.

Just as I was leaving, Nysa called out.

'Sweetheart, could you buy me a dozen macarons at the club? I need it for a cake I am making tomorrow.'

'Of course, darling, your wish is my command.' I bowed deeply in her direction and left her smiling.

Tennis was great fun, as always. The indoor courts at the Sports Complex of the club meant that we did not have to concern ourselves with the weather, so there were rarely any cancellations.

Raymond and I played against Chow Pin and Simon. They won, 6-2, 3-6, 6-4, but it was hard fought. I flubbed many of my first serves and was not happy that I was off my game. Too many errant thoughts floating around when I needed to focus.

After the usual exchange of insults and challenges in the locker room, I changed into a pair of jeans and a Polo shirt. I headed across to the Tea Room in the main club area to buy Nysa's macarons.

I chose the macarons and signed the bill as they were packing the pastry box.

Just as I was turning to head for the car park, I looked right.

Two men were walking into the lobby, talking to each other in low voices.

The first was an older (seventy or thereabouts) Chinese gentleman, impeccably dressed in 'smart casual'—ironed shorts, Polo shirt, multicoloured socks and walking shoes. His head was partially turned away from me.

The second was Greg Closier.

I stood there looking at him much like a deer in the headlights. He was deep in conversation with his companion and did not see me staring.

'Excuse me, sir.'

I looked back at the counter.

'Your macarons, sir,' said the young lady.

'Thank you very much, and have a good evening,' was my rote reply as I took the plastic bag that contained the box of macarons.

'Good evening, sir,' she said with a smile.

I stepped back from the counter and looked towards the lobby.

The two men had disappeared from sight.

I walked across to the lobby and looked around.

On my right was the club's main restaurant, The Olde Tavern. It was designed to mimic a cross between an English Pub and a Main Street restaurant. Low wattage lights gave it the ambience of a speakeasy.

I went to the restaurant and opened the door.

I had to squint and peer in the dim light.

Ah there. I saw Greg and his companion be seated at a table near the far windows. They continued to be deep in discussion.

'Good evening, sir,' said a voice, 'how may I help you?'

The head waiter stood there, regal in his black suit and bow tie.

'Ah, I have just come to order some food to take away,' I said. 'Could I sit down and have a drink while I wait?'

'Of course, sir,' he said, and turned to lead me to a table near the door. 'Would this table do?'

The table he pointed to was in a small alcove. The lack of a nearby lamp placed it in shadows.

'Perfect, thank you,' I said.

'I will get you a menu shortly. Would you like some water? Warm or iced?'

'Ice water please,' I said, placing my macarons on one chair and lowering myself on another.

'In just a minute, sir,' he said and left.

My chair faced the table that Greg was sitting at. He was facing in my direction, and while the lighting was subdued, I could see him clearly.

Both men were still speaking earnestly and continuously. They were totally engrossed.

A few moments later, I saw the head waiter leading a middle-aged Chinese lady to her table. She seemed to have come through the other door, on the far side of the restaurant. They passed Greg's table, crossing behind him, and went to one just beyond. The lady fussed with her handbag and umbrella and sat down. Her chair was just a couple of feet from Greg's and facing away from him. The head waiter stood patiently till she had settled down. They spoke a few words to each other, and he left.

I looked again towards Greg's table.

Another waiter stopped at their table to take their orders. They paused their conversation, picked up the menus and placed their orders. He jotted them down, collected the menus and stepped away. Greg and his visitor promptly resumed their discussion, Greg leaning forward and ticking off points on his fingers.

The restaurant was busy.

A young busboy came to my table and placed a glass of cold water on it. He handed me the rather elaborate menu.

'Thank you,' I said, 'please give me a few minutes to order.'

'Surely, sir,' he said and drifted off into the gloom.

I took stock of myself and the table.

I had my phone and wallet. And a bag containing macarons. The table had two napkins and two sets of cutlery—a fork, a knife and a spoon each.

I considered my next steps.

After three minutes, I took one of the napkins and put it into my jeans pocket. It was made of a silky fabric and did not bulge. I took the spoon, polished to a high sheen, and put it into my other pocket. I did this as unobtrusively as I could, but really did not have to worry. I am dark; I was wearing a navy-blue shirt and indigo-blue jeans. I was sitting in a poorly lit alcove. Unless someone was within five feet of me and was looking carefully, they would not even know I was there, leave alone see me stealing cutlery.

From time to time, I sipped my water and looked at my phone, just in case anyone was watching and wondered why someone was sitting still and motionless in the dark. Every two or three minutes, I would type something into my phone and then erase it.

Just then, another waiter came up to my table.

'Are you ready to order, sir?' he asked.

'So sorry, I need a few more minutes,' I said, 'I am waiting for my wife to confirm what she wants.'

He smiled as if he understood women. Fat chance.

'No problem, sir,' he said, 'please take your time.'

'If she doesn't decide soon, I am just going to leave,' I said, indicating long-suffering exasperation.

'No problem, sir,' he repeated, as he backed away.

Just as he left, I saw the waiter at Greg's table carry a laden tray and a tray stand. He stood the tray stand about four feet away, next to the Chinese lady's table, and placed the tray on it. He then turned around and walked back to the bar area, presumably to bring something more.

I looked at my phone to show any observer that I was not spying on Greg. I typed in the opening lines from two of my favourite books, and then erased them, and kept the phone down.

As I glanced up, I saw the Chinese lady from the table next to Greg's turn to the food tray. She seemed to be examining the selection, perhaps to decide her own order. Strangely, her hands seemed to be hovering just above the tray. I hoped she was not touching or tasting the food. Ugh.

After a couple of moments, she sat back, looked up and around, picked up the napkin on her table and wiped her hands. She then picked up her phone and scrolled through it.

Greg's waiter returned carrying a couple of ladles or spoons. He then began serving Greg and his companion.

When he finished, he spoke briefly to them. They barely glanced at him. He picked up the tray and the tray stand and went towards the kitchen area.

I looked away and took a sip of my water. I picked up my phone and unlocked it, preparing to type a few more words, but a movement caught my eye. The Chinese lady had got up and was walking away to the far side door. I looked down and typed the brands of six car manufacturers. Then I erased them.

Seven minutes passed. I was waiting for something, not sure exactly what.

I touched the spoon in my left pocket. It was still there.

The restaurant was buzzing. The bar was full. There was a group of four or five white men who were either celebrating or bemoaning the outcome of a football game. There was a lot of uproarious laughter and back slapping involved.

The waiter seemed to have forgotten that I was there. This suited me fine.

I looked over at Greg's table again. He seemed to be coughing and the other gentleman was peering with concern at him. They spoke briefly. Then Greg held on to the sides of the table and rose. He walked towards the door I was sitting next to, opened it and exited the restaurant into the main lobby. This was my chance, I thought.

I also arose. I picked up my phone and bag of macarons and stepped out.

I saw Greg cross the lobby and turn down the dog leg corridor that led to the restroom.

I followed.

CHAPTER 22

As I walked down the short corridor, my mind ran through various possibilities. Coldly, I reviewed each one and evaluated them. Discard, discard, keep, discard, may work, discard ...

I reached the men's restroom in less than fifteen seconds.

I stepped in. There was a small lobby, which opened to the main area on the right.

The restroom was empty. There was a line of sinks on my left, three urinals straight ahead, and a line of stalls on the right. There were four stalls, two of them were occupied. There was no one at the urinals or the sinks.

In one corner of the lobby was a small counter. I took the box of macarons out of the bag and placed the box on the counter. I took the plastic bag and moved towards the sinks.

I pulled out the napkin.

When we were children, there wasn't much in the way of entertainment. TVs were just about making their debut. Smart phones and tablets were decades away. So, we found new and interesting ways of keeping ourselves engaged and out of our parents' view.

This allowed us to learn all sorts of useful and useless skills. Kite-flying without falling off the roof, roller-skating on footpaths without face-planting, pavement-artistry using chalks that we stole from our school.

One of the things I learnt by accident when I was eleven years old was origami. A new family had moved into the cul de sac where we lived. The daughter, Betty, was about twenty and very pretty. Being adolescent boys, my two friends and I instantly had a crush on her. We did our best to strike up a conversation with her. We hung around outside her place, made up errands that would take us to her house, took a sudden interest in studies and went to her to get our doubts in physics and biology clarified. Betty was a real darling. She knew what we were up to and understood that it was our hormones directing all the stupid things we were doing.

One Saturday afternoon, Betty called the three of us in. We were thrilled. We had heard of how older women fancied younger men. We strutted in, excited and nervous. In the living room, we saw a bunch of newspapers and three pairs of scissors. We looked at one another. Was this some kind of exotic game that older women play?

Origami is the Japanese art of paper folding. You must have surely heard of it. The word originates from ori meaning 'folding', and kami meaning 'paper'. The goal is to transform a flat square sheet of paper into a finished sculpture through folding and sculpting techniques. You could take any piece of paper—newspaper, magazine page, napkin—and fold it into amazing shapes. A crane, a kite, a bag, a flower; anything was possible.

Over the next two weeks, Betty played Pygmalion to our Galatea. She channelled our raging hormones into focused creativity. The three of us started with an initial feeling of disappointment that she was not going to fulfil our wildest dreams. We ended trying to outdo each other in the complexity of our sculptures. Betty and those two weeks left me with a skill that I continually honed as I grew older, whilst sitting in boring meetings and airport lounges.

When Shahed was young, it was wonderful to see his eyes grow bigger and bigger as I fashioned shapes out of nothing but pieces of paper. He would keep some of the sculptures—the dinosaur, the eagle, the car—carefully on his bedside table till they fell, flew away or faded. As he grew up, I folded and sculpted less for him, but did not allow my skill to decay.

Strange, how something I learnt by accident five decades ago came in use today.

It took me all of twenty seconds to fashion a rudimentary glove. I slid that over my right hand to check. Yes, perfect fit.

I took it off again and kept it on the counter next to the left most sink. I kept the plastic bag beside it.

While this was happening, I heard sounds coming from the stalls.

One of the stall doors opened.

I turned the tap on and started washing my hands.

An older Chinese gentleman came out of the stall. He prepared to walk out of the restroom, then saw me, hesitated, and came to the right-most sink. He turned on the water, briefly dipped his hands in the stream and turned it off. He pulled five or six toilet tissues from the dispenser and wiped his hands and threw the tissues into the bin.

Then he turned and walked out without acknowledging me.

As soon as the door swung closed, I cupped my hands and filled them with water. I then turned to my right and sprinkled the floor. I did this once more. The floor was black marble, so the water droplets could not be easily spotted.

I turned off the tap, and quickly dried my hands on my jeans.

Another stall door opened. I turned on the tap but kept my hands dry. I glanced into the mirror.

Greg stepped out. He looked rather pale. A sheen of sweat covered his brow. That was strange, as the club usually overdid the air conditioning. I have had Canadians and Minnesotans complain about the cold.

He came to the sink and leaned on the counter with both hands, looking into the mirror at his pasty reflection. I don't think he even knew I was there. He took a couple of deep breaths.

I picked up the napkin-glove and put it on my right hand. I slipped my left hand into the plastic bag.

I took one step back and one to the right. This brought me to the left of, but slightly behind Greg.

With my left hand, through the plastic bag, I caught his left shirt sleeve. I brought my right hand just behind his head, above the nape of his neck.

In one motion, I pulled his left hand off the counter, and simultaneously pushed down on his head with all my strength.

Greg didn't resist. He couldn't. He was off-balance.

His head swung down hard and hit the edge of the sink. There was a subdued sound, like that of a watermelon falling and hitting the ground.

Greg crumpled. His legs folded and he collapsed to the floor, like a balloon that had deflated. He sprawled mostly on his right side, with his right arm partially under him and his left arm stretched out.

I took off the napkin-glove and shoved it into my pocket. I took the plastic bag, moved to the counter and put the box of macarons in it, and placed it again on the counter.

I turned on the tap and sprinkled some more water on the floor, near Greg's feet. I noted, to my satisfaction, that as he fell, Greg's shoes had left slide marks on the floor. *It certainly looks like he slipped on the wet floor,* I thought.

I shut off the water and wiped my hands on my jeans. I pulled out two tissues and wiped the tap clean. I pushed the tissues into my pocket.

I pulled out the spoon, bent down and held it below Greg's nose. The bright silvery metal did not fog. I put the spoon back in my pocket.

I took a final look. Greg's forehead had a deep crease in it. The skin around the crease was bright red. His eyes were partially open, looking at the wet floor tiles.

I turned around, picked up my macarons and left the restroom.

As I came around the corridor to the main lobby, I saw the old man who had not really washed his hands in the bathroom, sitting in an armchair across the lobby. He seemed to be waiting for someone.

As I walked across the lobby to the restaurant, someone brushed past me. It was the Chinese lady sitting at the table next to Greg's table.

'Excuse me,' I said, a little miffed.

She did not respond or even look back. I shook my head, entered the restaurant and went to my table. Some people, I thought. I unfolded the napkin and re-folded it to its original pattern. I kept it where it originally was. I placed the spoon in its former position.

I then walked to the head waiter. He was looking harried.

'Yes, sir,' he asked, when he saw me approach.

'I am so sorry, but my wife has already ordered food from elsewhere,' I said, 'I hope I haven't caused you any inconvenience.'

'Oh, not at all, sir,' he said, probably quite relieved, 'enjoy your dinner at home and I hope to see madam and you here soon.'

'Thank you so much,' I said. 'Have a good night.'

'Good night, sir.'

I left the restaurant through the other door. As I walked past Greg's table, I noticed his companion sipping on his wine and checking messages on his phone.

I came out on the patio, turned left and walked to the car park. As I walked, I lifted my left hand and looked at it. It was steady, or at least as steady as a sixty-year-old man's hand is. I transferred the bag of macarons to my left hand and looked at my right. Steady.

Not bad, I said to myself, as I reached my car and unlocked it. I put the macarons on the passenger seat.

I drove home.

CHAPTER 23

If you are shocked or horrified, I don't know what to say.

You should have seen this coming a long while ago.

What option did I have?

Should I have gone to Greg and said, 'Hey, could you please stop fucking my daughter-in-law? I would be really obliged?'

Or should I have complained to the government asking them to deport Greg and repatriate him to the UK under the Miscellaneous Offences Act?

Perhaps you think I should have prevailed upon Marianna's better instincts asking her to remember her wedding vows, discard her lover and pledge herself to loyalty and fidelity?

Did you not hear me when I said that I would need to sunder them permanently? The word 'permanently' means 'with zero possibility of any comebacks'.

There was only one way to make the separation permanent.

I had to kill Greg.

Then you may ask, don't you feel guilty? You just killed a man!

I thought about that.

Actually, I already spent many hours introspecting, asking myself that very question. Immediately after and in the days after. And the answer is, no, I still don't feel guilty.

I did what had to be done.

Remember, I am an asshole.

There is a school of thought that believes that you cannot be a CEO without being an asshole. (The transitive rule does not apply here—you can be an asshole and never be a CEO).

As a CEO, I have done far worse than killing Greg. I have fired people. I have downsized companies. I have flanked and undercut competing companies till they shut down and went away. I have paid large sums of money to motivate the right people not to look closely at environmental reports that detail the harm our products were causing. I have compromised employees in other companies and bought industrial secrets. Are these any worse than murder?

Do retrenched employees go home and tell their spouses, 'I was let go today. I truly deserved it. The company did the right thing to survive. I must now do penitence for my sins'?

Does the owner of a company that has to shut down (because I undercut him out of business) tell his wife, 'The business that my father built and handed over to me is gone. But on reflection, I realise that I deserve it. I did not adapt to changing times. I hope you don't mind leaving this condo and moving to a 3-room HDB.'

What did Charles Darwin say? When push comes to shove, we need to do what we need to do. Survival of the fittest, of those who are willing to do what it takes, everyone else be damned.

Either you are a sheep or a wolf. I never belonged in a herd.

Next, you will want to know how I slept after committing such a heinous act.

Would it pacify you if I said that I tossed and turned, sweating profusely, hideous images of the fires of hell burning my retinas every time I closed my eyes?

Sorry to disappoint. I slept soundly. No bad dreams, no soaked sheets, no demonic visions.

Have we finally got all this moral nonsense out of the way?

Now, if you will allow me, I need to review everything, to ensure that I did not make any mistakes or leave a trail to follow.

One, Greg and I did not know each other. We had never met. I don't think he knew I existed. The only connection between us, Marianna, was quite tenuous.

Two, at the club, I had not interacted with Greg. No one saw us together.

Three, I did not touch Greg. I made sure to use a makeshift glove on my right hand and a plastic bag on my left. Also, I did not touch anything in the restroom other than the tap, which I wiped clean.

Four, there was no record of my being in the restaurant. I did not purchase anything or swipe my membership card. And it was a busy night, so I doubt that anybody there, the head waiter or the waiter who served me water, would remember my fleeting presence.

Five, my presence *was* registered in the club that day, but on the tennis court and in the Tea Room, when I bought the macarons. However, the time stamps should show that it was well before Greg was found.

Six, I was not in the club when the body was found. I don't even know when it was found.

However ...

I hate 'howevers'. Ever since my first report card in first grade.

My class teacher, Mrs Kambatta, always started off by writing so many nice things.

'Ishmael is such a bright boy.'

'He leads the class in Arithmetic.'

'Ishmael's reading skills are that of a third grader.'

Then, instead of finishing with, 'Ishmael's parents must praise him and give him ice cream every day,' she wrote,

'*However*, Ishmael talks a lot in class and distracts his classmates. He must learn to be more disciplined.'

Guess which of these statements my parents latched on to?

Since then, 'howevers' have been the bane of my existence.

However, one person did see me in the vicinity of Greg. The old Chinese gentleman who was using a stall in the bathroom (and who did not really wash his hands). He also saw me when I exited the restroom area.

Would he put two and two together? After all, both sightings were brief and he had not seen Greg, had he?

However, if there were cameras in the car park, they would show that I actually left after Greg's demise.

Would the police find that suspicious?

I filed away both these facts. There was nothing I could do about them for now.

By the time I reached home, I had completed my review. I would do a more detailed one later, but for now, I was reasonably confident that there was nothing that could link me directly to Greg's passing.

I reached our condo, parked and sat in the car for two minutes. I looked at my smart watch. My resting heart rate showed its usual 48 beats per minute. I felt inordinately pleased with that reading.

'Hi Nysa,' I called out when I entered our apartment. 'I'm home!'

'Coming, darling,' she called back from inside, 'just a minute ...'

At the front door, I took off my shoes. I went into the guest wash closet and pulled out a couple of wet wipes. I wiped the shoes clean, uppers and soles. I leaned them against the wall to dry out.

Then I went to the dining room, pulled out the box of macarons from the plastic bag and put it on the dining table. I crumpled the plastic bag and threw it down the garbage chute. Next, I pulled off my sweaty tennis clothes in the utility room, draped myself in a towel and dropped them into the sink. I rinsed them in a small bucket, soaped them and put them in the washing machine.

Just as I was exiting the utility room, Nysa came in.

'So, how was your game?' asked Nysa.

'Great game, and really tiring,' I smiled at her. 'The teams were evenly matched and there were many really long rallies.'

'Good,' she smiled back, 'but did you win or lose?'

'Lost,' I said, ruefully, 'but only by a whisker.'

'Poor thing,' she said, giving me a kiss, 'Now are you ready for dinner?'

'More than ready,' I said, moving to the dining table.

'Hey, go wash your hands! And put something decent on!'

'Yes, ma'am,' I said, and walked to our bathroom to do as told.

As I said, I slept soundly that night. Nary a nightmare.

Interlude 7 – Shahed, Determined

Tomorrow, I am going to hash this out with Marianna.

I am sick of this feeling, that something is wrong. That there is a cloud hanging over us, our relationship. There are unsaid things. Our paths seem to be diverging.

I have been thinking continuously this last week.

Yes, I want to be the General Manager of the APAC region. It would be fun and validating. But not at the cost of our relationship. No. I love Marianna too much to imagine life without her.

I remember, in Bible Studies, Sister Margaret sharing the question, 'What doth it profit a man, to gain the whole world, and lose his own soul?'

If I lost Marianna, I would have as well lost my soul.

I would have done this tonight, but she is off with her friends for a birthday party.

I am going to sit her down and ask her what she wants. Ask her why she seems so distracted and occupied all the time. Why she is out of the office so often and late home almost every night. Why she doesn't seem to want to do the things we have always done together anymore.

I am scared, shit scared of what her answers are likely to be.

Even now, I am saying all this after my fourth beer. Dutch courage. From a German beer.

I have made a note of all the points I want to discuss. She always laughs at me when she sees me doing this, but I feel much more prepared and confident when I have everything written down.

I have made sure that neither she nor I have any other plans for tomorrow. It's a Sunday and we are both at home. No interruptions, no sudden calls from the office.

Should I talk to Mom? She is the most sensible person I know. She will know what to say and how to say it.

Let's see. I will decide on that tomorrow morning, it's late now and I don't want to worry her unnecessarily.

I know that I have already let my guard down with Dad. But he keeps things to himself. He is not the best advisor on relationships, is he? He tends to be much more binary than fuzzy. All or nothing. No shades of grey. But hey, Mom and he have been married for more than thirty-five years and they clearly love each other, so what do I know?

Okay enough beer, I am getting maudlin.

Tomorrow is the day.

CHAPTER 24

The next morning, I woke up with a sense of unusual well-being. A feeling of quiet achievement.

I stretched and decided to stay in bed for a few more minutes.

But that was not to be.

'Ishmael, are you awake?' Nysa called from outside our bedroom.

I declined to answer on the grounds that it would incriminate me.

'Ishmael!' her voice was getting closer.

I pulled the covers over my head. I wanted to bask in these nice feelings that I hadn't felt since I retired.

Nysa entered the bedroom.

'Ishmael, get up,' she said urgently.

I pulled the covers off grumpily.

'What? Can a man not sleep in peace?'

'Ishmael,' said Nysa. Her voice broke a little.

I sat up.

'What is the matter, sweetheart?' I asked. 'Are the kids okay?'

'Oh Ishmael, Marianna's boss has been murdered!'

'What? Who?' I asked, inserting the right amount of alarm in my voice. 'When? Where?'

These four questions are integral to the path of all knowledge.

'One of the senior partners in her company,' said Nysa. 'A person named Greg something. And Ishmael, it seems he was killed in our club!'

I got off the bed and went to hold Nysa.

'Oh God,' I said, 'when did this happen? I was at the club last night!'

'I don't know when or how,' said Nysa. 'I just spoke to Marianna. She was crying so much, I could barely understand what she was saying!'

Of course, she was crying. No more afternoon trysts. No more forbidden fruit.

'Did you speak to Shahed?' I asked. 'He may know something more.'

'No, I just wanted to let you know,' she said. 'What should we do? Should I go over to Marianna's?'

'Give me a few minutes,' I said. 'Let me wash up and speak to Shahed, and then we can decide what to do.'

That is what I did. Brushed my teeth, washed my face and called Shahed.

'I can't believe it,' he said, in lowered tones. 'A murder? In Singapore? And in the Tangerine Club of all places?'

'Do you know what happened? And when?'

'Not too much, Dad,' said Shahed. 'Sometime last evening, it seems. Greg had gone there for dinner with a client or somebody, and someone killed him there.'

'How is Marianna?' I asked, more out of courtesy than anything else.

'She is devastated,' he replied. 'He was her direct boss. She worked under him.'

And did other things under him, I thought.

'Should Mom and I come over?' I asked.

'Not now,' he said, 'but thank you. Can I call after an hour and let you know?'

'Sure, Shahed,' I said, 'we are here. Whatever you need.'

Nysa was listening, wide-eyed.

I updated her on what Shahed had said.

'Oh my God,' she said, her hand at her throat, 'what a tragedy!'

'There's nothing we can do for now,' I said. 'Let's wait for Shahed's call.'

I held her tightly for a few moments.

'Okay,' she sighed, 'let me finish my chores so that I am ready to leave if they need us.'

She stepped out of my embrace and left the bedroom.

I went to the credenza and took my phone off the charger.

My WhatsApp screen showed a riot of messages.

'OMG!'

'Murder? In the club?'

'What is Singapore coming to?'

'Who is this Greg? Does anyone know him?'

'Some bigshot lawyer, I believe!'

'They say he was beaten to death!'

'Oh, I heard he was stabbed!'

'The management should resign! What a shame!'

I sat on the settee, reading the outpourings.

As I did, I tingled with a sense of excitement. And achievement.

I abruptly kept the phone down beside me.

What was happening? First, I wake up feeling good. Now, I read about a man's death—which I caused—and I feel better. I needed to explore and understand this.

I quickly changed into my running gear.

'Nysa,' I said, walking into the living room where she was immersed in her phone, 'I am going for a run. I will be back in an hour or so.'

'Oh,' she said, looking up, 'what if Shahed calls?'

'He will call me also,' I said reassuringly, 'I will turn around and come back immediately, then we can go over.'

'Okay, take care,' said Nysa, her head swivelling back to her phone.

I ignored the elevator and ran down the stairs. As soon as I reached the lobby, I set off on a brisk jog, turning left out of the gate and heading towards Kallang River.

Why was I feeling so good?

Yes, I realised that I had achieved my objective of ensuring that Marianna's affair was shut down. No Greg, no affair.

That meant that Shahed's marriage was safe—for the time being—and that gave me reassurance.

But that was just bringing our family back to square one, before I found out about Marianna.

What else had changed?

I started reviewing the events in my life, going back a month at a time.

As I ran past Ophir Road, a car slowed down and someone waved me on. I smiled and waved at him, thanking the driver for his courtesy.

As I parsed and analysed, a few synapses, so far dormant, started firing.

When I was working, there was a sense of mission, a sense of purpose. Each day was an attempt to move towards an agreed goal.

When I was working, there was a sense of being needed. Of being looked up to. Of being consulted and listened to.

When I was working, A led to B, which led to C. There was a sense of creating something. A feeling of progress.

Since I retired, things had changed.

Yes, life was good. It was restful. I had enough time to do what I wanted to do.

But it was mostly vanilla, not Rocky Road. There was no crunch, no chew. Vanilla is a pleasant taste, but not an exciting one.

As I turned into the river park, I realised that over the last year, I had had no purpose. I was drifting along aimlessly and amiably down the gentle currents of time, no more steering my boat, but being steered by the river's flow.

Any progress I made was not mine. It was made by events and people for me.

I realised that I was not needed any more. Nysa had her life, her friends, her daily and weekly routines. I figured in some of them but was more of a prop than a player. Shahed and Marianna led their own lives. Sometimes their lives intersected and overlapped with ours but more as ships passing each other than heading to the same port.

I noted dispassionately that I was not really adding or creating any value since I retired. Yes, I was consulting a little, mentoring a few people, but those were minor contributions with limited impact.

Then, as I neared the stadium, I had a small Eureka moment.

I had become irrelevant.

I stopped, my heart pounding, not just because of the run.

All that was true, I thought, as I stood by the river and looked at its turgid waters.

I had stopped doing, I was not creating any value. Nobody needed me.

I was not relevant anymore.

It hit me suddenly why so many of my contemporaries refused to let go of their jobs. They were desperately trying to retain their relevance, their reason for being.

Was that why I was feeling so good?

Had I found a new reason to exist? Was a new purpose dawning?

I checked my phone. No update from Shahed yet.

I checked my watch. Five and a half kilometres. Enough.

I turned around and headed back home.

CHAPTER 25

At 11.30 a.m., Nysa and I left for Shahed's place.

Their condo was on Paterson Road, and we reached within ten minutes.

Shahed buzzed us in and met us at their apartment door. He was unshaven and still in his pyjamas. His face was strained.

Nysa pulled him in and gave him a fierce hug. He lay his head on hers and stood like that for a while.

Then, he reached out to me and brought me into the fold.

There wasn't much to say, was there?

As we moved from the foyer to the living room, we heard Marianna sobbing.

'She has been crying since the morning,' said Shahed softly.

I bet.

Nysa surged forward and went to Marianna who was sitting on the sofa, her head in her hands.

Marianna looked up.

'Nysa!' she wailed and stood up and fell into Nysa's arms. Nysa held her and murmured into her ears.

Shahed and I stood there for a few moments.

'Let's go into the family room,' he suggested. I nodded and we moved away, leaving Nysa to console Marianna.

Shahed sat on the arm of the settee.

'Do you know what happened?' I asked. 'How did you find out?'

'Richard Lee called at about 7 a.m.,' he said. 'Richard is the Managing Partner. It seems Jocelyn called him last night, around 11 p.m. Richard was at Jocelyn's place the whole night.'

'So, what happened?' I prompted.

'It seems Greg went for dinner with a client to the club,' he said. 'Sometime during the dinner, Greg was not feeling too well and went to the restroom. After a few minutes, when he didn't return, the client went towards the restroom to check. Just then, he heard a commotion and a couple of members came rushing out calling for the manager.'

'Mm-hmm,' I said.

'There was a lot of confusion,' said Shahed, 'but long story short, Greg was hit on the head or fell on his head, or something. The police were there within ten minutes, and they sealed off the area, calling it a crime scene.'

'My God,' I murmured.

'Then the club called Jocelyn, who called Richard, and they were there till midnight,' Shahed continued. 'After that the police took Greg away for an autopsy, Jocelyn and Richard went back to Greg's place. That's all I have so far.'

'This is truly tragic,' I said, arranging my face into the appropriate configuration.

'Yes, Marianna is devastated,' he said, his face a mix of many emotions, none of which I could read. 'She and Greg seem to have been closer than I knew. I thought they were just colleagues …'

I was glad he didn't know the extent of their closeness.

'She kept saying something about "all our plans for the future",' he said, his voice full of misery. He looked at me, 'I don't know, Dad, but there seems to be more to this than …'

I put my arm around him.

'People say all sorts of things in the throes of grief, Shahed,' I said. 'Wait till she calms down. No point conjecturing without knowing.'

'Yeah, I guess you are right,' he said, rubbing his face.

'Why don't you go have bath?' I suggested. 'Have you had anything to drink or eat?'

'No. I would love a coffee, though.'

'Okay, go freshen up and I will make coffee for all of you,' I said.

'Thank you, Dad,' he said gratefully, walking towards their bedroom.

I went into their postage stamp kitchen. It took me a few minutes to figure out how to operate their state-of-the-art coffee maker which hissed and spat at me before finally cooperating. I poured three mugs of coffee and took them on a tray into the living room.

Marianna seemed a little calmer now. She sat next to Nysa, holding hands.

'Coffee?' I asked.

'Oh, thank you, Ishmael,' said Marianna, accepting a mug. Nysa took another, and I kept the tray on the centre table for Shahed.

'Shahed has gone for a shower,' I said, 'perhaps …'

Nysa glanced at me. It was her 'please keep quiet' glare. I subsided and quietly stood leaning against the wall.

A minute later, Shahed came in, looking refreshed. He picked up the third mug.

'Thank you, Dad,' he said, sitting in the armchair across the sofa.

Nysa and I stayed till 2 p.m. Nysa had taken charge and made a simple lunch—French Toast and Coleslaw—that we ate, largely in silence. Marianna had bathed and was responding to texts and calls.

'We need to go to Jocelyn's house,' she told Shahed, just as we were finishing lunch. 'Are you okay if we go now?'

'Of course,' he said.

'Dad and I will leave, too,' said Nysa, 'Give us a call once you are back.'

Marianna rose from the table and embraced Nysa, and then me.

'Thank you for always being there for us,' she said, her eyes filling up with tears again.

Nysa held her for a few moments.

'Always,' she said.

We returned home exhausted. Grief does that to you, you know. It sucks up the life force.

'I am going to lie down for a while,' said Nysa.

'Me, too,' I said. 'Also, I have tennis at 5 p.m. at the club. I hope it's okay if I play?'

Nysa considered this for a moment.

'Yes, I don't see why not,' she said. 'If they call, I will go over and you can join later.'

We lay down. Nysa slept and I read. I couldn't sleep. The coil of excitement continued to uncurl within me.

At 4.40 p.m., I arose, changed into my tennis gear and left for the club.

The other three members of our foursome were already there when I arrived. We greeted each other, but instead of starting our normal warm-up routine, we spoke about the killing. Each of them had 'absolutely first-hand information straight from the horse's mouth' and knew nothing. The conversation was mostly cathartic—these were all wealthy and well-connected men, insulated from most seamier parts of life, not at all accustomed to having death deposited on their doorstep.

'I am not going into the club bathrooms or locker rooms anymore,' said Chow Pin, half in jest, but fear lurked in his eyes.

'We need more security guards,' said Raymond, 'safety has to be the first priority!'

'The police in this country is going downhill fast,' averred Simon, with conviction.

It took fifteen minutes of gentle ushering onto the court before we finally started to play.

The games were great fun, as always. We were evenly matched and played to win.

At one point in the second set, I noticed three people in the viewing gallery, watching us. It wasn't clear, but there was something familiar about the one standing apart. Then Raymond served, and I got back into the game.

'Fantastic game!' said Raymond, at 6.55 p.m., as we finished. '6-4, 3-6, 7-5! Every point could have gone either way!'

'Yes,' said Chow Pin, 'your serves are amazing, Raymond. You had what, six or seven aces?'

'Yeah, but Ishmael sends every ball back regardless!' exclaimed Simon, Raymond's partner today. 'Bloody Energiser Bunny!'

We all laughed. A good game trumps murder every time.

We picked up fresh towels and went into the locker room. No one thought to look over their shoulder.

I checked my messages. Nothing from Nysa so far.

'I am heading in for a shower, guys,' I said, 'see you on Saturday.'

We chorused our goodbyes.

The hot water pulsed some energy back into my depleted body. I towelled off and stepped into the changing room.

I was alone, except for one person standing near the far wall. I continued to my locker.

'Excuse me,' he said.

I turned around.

It was the Chinese gentleman from the restroom the previous night. The one who had not washed his hands properly.

'Yes?' I asked, disquiet trickling into my veins.

'May I have a word with you?' he asked, politely.

CHAPTER 26

I looked at him.

He could have been anything between fifty-five and seventy years old. He was slim, almost thin, about my height. He was wearing a cream half-sleeved shirt neatly tucked into a pair of dark grey formal pleated pants. Rather oddly, he was wearing white running shoes. That was a bit jarring.

'And you are?' I asked.

'My name is Lee,' he said.

'And what is this regarding?' I asked.

'I think you know what this is regarding, Mr Dollah,' he said.

'No, I don't,' I responded, rather sharply.

'Do you really want to do this here?' asked Lee. 'Wouldn't it be better to go somewhere a little more private? Perhaps to the coffee shop upstairs?'

I looked around. We were alone for the moment. However, someone could step in at any time.

'Okay,' I nodded. 'But not upstairs.' I thought for a moment. 'How about the BreadTalk in Scotts Square?'

'Yes, I know it,' he nodded. He looked at his watch. 'Shall we meet there at 7.45 p.m.?'

'Sure,' I said. I opened my locker and pulled out my clothes. As I started dressing, Lee made his way out. I pulled on my jeans and t-shirt, pushed my feet into my slip-ons, picked up my tennis bag and left the changing room.

As I walked to the car, my brain went into overdrive.

So, Lee had put two and two together. And come to the right conclusion. He knew that I was involved somehow in Greg's death.

The fact that he had approached me indicated that he was probably not an upright citizen. If he were, he should have spoken to the police. Or the club management, who would have told the police.

So, the question was, what did he want? Actually, two questions—what did he have, and what did he want.

I reached my car and got in.

While buckling in, I did a quick check of my internal processes. To my surprise, and consequent satisfaction, I realised that I was not afraid. On the contrary, I felt a sense of anticipation. Of expectancy; like I was standing at the baseline waiting for my opponent to serve, eyes focused on the blob of yellow, every muscle and tendon ready to pounce, to send the ball careening back down the line beyond anyone's reach.

I took a deep breath and started the car. Let the games begin, I thought, and smiled.

I entered Scotts Square at 7.40 p.m. I went down the escalator and walked into BreadTalk. Lee hadn't arrived yet. The place was empty. I stepped up to the counter.

'Good evening,' I said, to the assistant. 'Are you open?'

'Till eight o'clock only,' he said, wiping down the display case.

'Thank you,' I said. I found a table at the far corner and sat down on a chair against the wall. As I did, Lee walked in. He saw me and came up to me.

'Would you like some coffee?' he asked politely.

'No, thank you,' I said, equally suave. 'I don't drink coffee or tea. You please go ahead.'

'No, that is okay,' he said, pulling out the chair opposite me and sitting down.

There was silence for a few moments.

'Well, Mr Lee, this is your meeting,' I said, sitting back with one arm on the chair next to mine.

He leaned forward, his elbows on the table, his hands clasped.

'You see, Mr Dollah, I saw you in the club restroom last night. And I saw you come out. I was waiting for a friend in the lobby. I had clear visibility of the restroom area. No one else went in after you came out till Mr Warner went in and came out in a panic.'

'Mm-hmm,' I said.

'The police are saying that Mr Closier was killed,' he said.

'Mm-hmm.' I said.

'You see how this places me in a quandary,' he said.

'Not really,' I said. 'How does it place you in any kind of quandary?'

'Come on, Mr Dollah,' he said, 'we are both men of the world. If I went to the police, this would create so many complications—for you, for the club, for your family …'

The feeling of expectancy stirred and bared its teeth.

I smiled.

'Are you accusing me of anything, Mr Lee?' I asked, pleasantly.

He sat back.

'No, no, not at all,' he said, 'after all, I wasn't there. I don't know what happened. I only know that you were there, and perhaps the police would benefit from your help in investigating the case.'

The man had a silver tongue, to be sure.

'And what is stopping you from going to the police and sharing with them all that you saw?' I asked.

'We are fellow members of the club, Mr Dollah,' he said earnestly. 'Why should I cause a fellow member any trouble? Or even our club? I have been a member for more than thirty years. I don't want to cause the club any trouble.'

'I see,' I said. I sat silent for a few seconds.

'I just thought we could reach an understanding between us. A gentleman's agreement,' continued Mr Lee, filling the silence with words.

'Mm-hmm,' I said.

'What do you say, Mr Dollah?' he asked, impatience creeping into his voice.

'What form would this understanding take, Mr Lee?' I asked.

He leant forward again.

'You see, Mr Dollah,' he said sincerely, 'I am in a bit of a financial bind and need some help. If you could afford me this help, then I don't need to find it anywhere else. Both our problems disappear.'

'I see,' I said, not surprised. 'How much do you need to extricate yourself from this problem?'

For the first time, Mr Lee looked a little abashed. Blackmail was new to him, I think.

'I need about fifty thousand dollars,' he said, 'I can pay off my debts and …'

He looked at me to see the impact of the sum on me.

'That is a lot of money, Mr Lee,' I said.

He made an attempt to smile reassuringly.

'You have been a CEO of many companies, Mr Dollah,' he said, relaying that he had been quite busy on social media since last night. 'Fifty thousand dollars should not be an issue for you, I think.'

Just then, the shop assistant came up to us.

'Closing now, any last order?' he asked, clearly wanting us to leave.

'No, thank you,' I replied, 'we will be leaving shortly.'

I rose from my chair.

'I will take your offer under advisement, Mr Lee,' I said, 'I will need to think about it.'

He rose too.

'This offer has a very limited shelf life,' he said, almost threateningly. 'How long will you need?'

'I will contact you on Tuesday morning,' I said, 'please give me your phone number.'

He rattled off his number. I keyed it into my phone but did not make a call. I did not want any evidence of his number on my phone.

'I will call you on Tuesday before lunch,' I said.

'Thank you, Mr Dollah,' he said. 'I sincerely hope we can resolve this problem like gentlemen. If I don't hear from you ...'

'You will,' I said.

I started walking towards the FairPrice store. I did not want to walk with Lee to the escalator. The silence would have been quite awkward.

Interlude 8 – Marianna, Devastated

Oh My God!

What happened? How?

This is such a disaster, such a tragedy!

Greg is dead.

I can't believe it.

Just last Monday we were in office together. We were supposed to meet at the hotel on the coming Tuesday.

I can't believe Greg is dead.

What am I going to do?

Everything we were planning for, everything we were going to do together is gone. Vanished. Lost.

Who could have killed him? Greg was a corporate lawyer, for God's sake. He didn't harm anyone. He advised on mergers and acquisitions and takeovers. He dealt with contracts, escrow accounts and closings.

Poor Jocelyn. I can't bear to see her like this. She hasn't stopped crying since we came. I am so glad that there are people around her. I have no idea what I should say if we were alone. What is she going to do? How is she going to manage?

What am *I* going to do now?

I can't talk to anyone about Greg and me. About what we were planning together. Nobody would understand.

I wish I could speak to Shahed. He is the only person I can truly trust to understand. But he seems distant. There seems to be a chasm between us. I don't understand why. We normally speak to each other all the time, but over the past few weeks, it's as if he is avoiding talking to me.

I can't deal with Shahed now, in this state of mind. I might say something I can't take back.

Oh, God, why did this happen to us?

What am I going to do now?

CHAPTER 27

As I traced my steps to my car, I opened my phone. I had taken two photos of Lee when he approached me at BreadTalk. They were quite clear.

I drove back to the club.

I walked over to the reception.

'Hi, Kumar, good evening,' I said to the manager on duty.

'Good evening, Mr Dollah, how are you?' he said, smiling brightly. He and I have known each other for many years, and I have helped him in a couple of matters in the past.

'Very well, thank you,' I said. 'You look well. How is the family?'

'Very good, sir. My son just completed his O levels and has done quite well,' he said, beaming proudly.

'Shripad is a bright young man, and will make you proud,' I said.

'How may I help you?' he asked.

'Do you know this gentleman, Kumar?' I asked, showing him Lee's photo.

'Ah yes, sir, this is Mr Lee Sun Wah,' replied Kumar without hesitation. 'He has been a member here for many years.'

'Oh, thank you, Kumar,' I said. 'You see, I was introduced to him at a party, and couldn't recall his name. Growing old, you see.'

We both laughed.

'I won't take any more of your time, Kumar,' I said, 'take care, and give your son my congratulations.'

'Sure, sir, my pleasure,' said Kumar.

Lee Sun Wah.

I drove home, greeted Nysa and sat down for dinner with her.

'Shahed and Marianna haven't called,' said Nysa, 'I think they are still at Jocelyn's.'

'Yes,' I nodded, 'they'll probably be there for a while, till the situation settles a little.'

'Greg's family must be devastated,' she said, mournfully. 'How can something like this happen, that too in the club, in Singapore?'

'Low crime does not mean no crime,' I said, quoting one of Singapore's favourite aphorisms.

'Ishmael!' said Nysa, sharply, 'don't be facile. This is not the time.'

'Sorry, sweetheart,' I said, 'I don't know how to react to death, never have.'

We continued with our meal but my mind was already in the study. As soon as I finished eating and clearing up, I followed it there.

For the next hour and half, I extracted everything I could about Lee.

68 years old. Retired banker. Lived on Barker Road in a landed property with his much younger second wife. Estranged from his first wife and son. He didn't seem to have any hobbies, had a marginal social presence and was quite unremarkable.

There was a lot more but nothing relevant to my objectives.

I turned the chair, put my feet on the settee and leaned back.

My sense of anticipation was steadily building into excitement.

I calmed myself down. I could not afford to make any more mistakes—the call to Nestor & Ross was enough.

How should I handle this?

I visualised and explored options till Nysa called me to bed.

For two hours after Nysa nodded off to sleep, I listened to her steady breathing and continued reviewing my options.

Finally, my exertions on the tennis court caught up with me and I slept.

I woke up on Monday morning, bright and early, with a spring in my step. Nysa was still fast asleep. I went into the bathroom, brushed, washed and put on my running gear.

I drove to MacRitchie Reservoir and parked. Then I took my phone, walked for a couple of hundred metres and started jogging.

As I ran, I was looking for a particular spot. I had seen it before on my runs. About 600 metres in, I slowed down and stopped. There, on my right, was a bench. It was tucked away behind a couple of young trees, overlooking the reservoir. I looked around the bench to confirm that my memory was right—there were no lamp posts nearby.

I walked to the bench and looked back at the path. The low hanging foliage made it difficult to peer through.

I looked across the reservoir. The opposite bank was at least seven hundred metres away and had trees to the edge.

I continued inspecting the space from every angle, physical and functional, till I was satisfied.

I stepped back on the path and resumed my run.

Seventy-eight minutes later, I was back at the car, soaking wet and gasping. I towelled myself down, placed the towel on the seat and drove home.

Nysa met me at the door.

'Ishmael, Shahed called about half hour ago. He asked if we could come over and spend some time with them,' she said.

'Of course,' I said, 'give me fifteen minutes, I will change and be ready to leave.'

We were at their condo by 9.20 a.m.

Shahed let us in. He looked really tired.

'Hi Mom, hi Dad,' he said, 'come on in.'

Nysa gave him her customary hug.

'Where is Marianna? How is she?' she asked.

'She is in the bath,' he said, 'she is still in shock. Yesterday was brutal, having a colleague murdered like that. We came back home from Jocelyn's only around midnight.

'How was it?' I asked. 'Did Jocelyn have her family with her?'

'I think so, yes. There were so many people coming and going,' he said. 'Jocelyn was in shock, for quite a while she didn't know what was going on around her. Later, she seemed to calm down a little.'

'And then there were the police—some detectives from the CID, I think,' he continued. 'They were asking a lot of questions and searched the house. Jocelyn's mother said that they focused on the kitchen, the pantry and the bathrooms. Why do you suppose?'

I shook my head.

'I can't imagine why,' I said, genuinely mystified. Were they looking for a kitchen implement to explain the crease in Greg's forehead? But they should have matched it to the contour of the sink. I shrugged.

'Did you get enough rest, Shahed?' asked Nysa, not bothered about who searched for what, where.

'Not really, Mom,' he said, 'once we came home, we couldn't sleep. Marianna needed me beside her. I think we drifted off to sleep by 3 a.m. or so.'

'Poor boy,' said Nysa, 'I hope you are not going into the office today?'

'I don't need to go but Marianna says she has to,' he said. 'She asked me if I could come with her.'

Just then Marianna entered the living room.

She looked wan and woebegone.

She walked up to Nysa and accepted her hug. They stood like that for a while.

'Thank you for coming,' said Marianna. 'Can I make you some coffee or tea?'

'What did both of you eat last night?' asked Nysa.

'Ah, there were some sandwiches laid out at Jocelyn's,' said Marianna, 'I didn't have the heart to eat. Did you have some, Shahed?' she turned and asked.

'Not really, no,' he confessed.

'Both of you sit down,' ordered Nysa, 'I'll whip up something quickly. You need to keep up your strength.'

She went into the kitchen.

Marianna, Shahed and I sat in the living room. Each of us were lost in our own thoughts.

Marianna raised her eyes and looked at me.

'Why would the CID search Greg's kitchen and bathrooms?' she asked.

'Shahed asked the same question, my dear,' I said, 'I really can't think of why. If the death occurred at home, they could be searching for the cause of death, but he passed on at the club. I don't understand why.'

She picked up her phone and started scanning her messages.

Fifteen minutes later, Nysa came into the living room, with two steaming plates of scrambled eggs and toast, and two mugs of coffee.

'Eat,' she commanded, and they did.

At 11.30 a.m., Marianna and Shahed went into their bedroom to change. They came out a few minutes later. All of us left their apartment and took the elevator down to the basement car park. There, we said our goodbyes and agreed to meet for dinner at our place that evening.

'Call us anytime, if you need anything at all,' I told Shahed, pulling him aside before he got into the car. He nodded and gave me a brief hug.

Nysa and I drove back home.

As we alighted from the car in our car park, she looked at me.

'What is this going to do to them?' she asked. 'Will this bring them together or pull them apart?'

Her eyes were frightened and her face was tight with worry.

I had absolutely no idea. The moving finger has written, and having done so, moves on.

Segue 3 – Ishmael's Notebook

— *November:*

Task 1:
~~To confirm the allegations.~~
   1. ~~How can I confirm the allegations?~~
   2. ~~What resources did I have at my disposal?~~
   3. ~~What tactics best fit this situation?~~
DONE.

Task 2:
~~To separate Marianna and Greg.~~
   1. ~~How do I find out everything about Greg?~~
   2. ~~Where and how do I accost / confront him?~~
   3. ~~What approach would ensure a permanent separation between him and Marianna?~~
DONE.

Task 3:
Lee Sun Wah—to mitigate threat

1. Is he a concern or a problem?
2. What is the best approach?

Follow on notes:
1. Info on Lee
   a. Club?
   b. Social media?
   c. Do I need to track?
2. Approach?
   a. TBD

CHAPTER 28

Nysa and I went up to the apartment, she sad and tired, and I chafing at the bit.

Siti had made lunch. We ate desultorily. Nysa just picked at her food. That is the problem with being empathetic. You first sense and then carry others' sorrows on your shoulders. For no valid reason. With no material outcome. I am glad I am tone deaf to most emotions.

After lunch, I requested leave of Nysa, saying that I needed to complete some errands. I drove to the Botanical Gardens and parked at the Nassim Road car park.

I walked towards the Jacob Ballas Garden.

On the way, about 400 metres in, I stopped at a slight rise. There were a set of steps, mossy and unused. I climbed them and came into a small clearing within a thicket of trees. Here was another bench I had noticed during my past wanderings.

I examined the area carefully. No lights. No cameras. Difficult to see from the pathway. Not used very much—the bench, too, was quite worn and tired.

I walked around the area, looking for anything that might disqualify it as a site for a private meeting place. There was no veto.

I completed my review and walked back to the car, got in and drove home.

When I walked into the living room, Nysa was busy on her laptop.

I bent over and kissed her head. She looked up and smiled.

'Sweetheart, do we have any chopsticks?' I asked.

She frowned.

'Yes, I think so, in the credenza in the dining room, top drawer,' she said, 'but why do you need chopsticks?'

'I am carrying out a small repair on my briefcase, and need a hardy rod,' I explained. 'Are these wood or plastic?'

'I can't remember, Ishmael,' she replied, 'could you please check for yourself? I need to complete this task today. I am already late because of, you know ...'

'No worries,' I said and went to the dining room.

I found the chopsticks. There were quite a few sets, mostly stolen from restaurants across Singapore (and a couple from Malaysia). I pulled out one set and tested it. I tried bending it, then breaking it, but it resisted my efforts heroically.

Good. I took both the sticks and went to the study. On the way, I picked up my tool kit from the utility room.

I spent the next hour preparing them for what I had in mind.

At about 4.30 p.m., I came into the kitchen and rummaged through the fridge. I was looking for a hard-boiled egg, some tomatoes or grapes. I found all three and took them to the study and continued my preparations.

At about 5.15 p.m., I heard the doorbell ring.

Ah, that must be Marianna and Shahed, I thought.

I put away my tool kit and the modified chop sticks. I quickly ate the remains of the egg, the tomato and the grapes (though there was not much left of the latter). I wiped the place clean and dry.

By the time I reached the living room, Nysa had ushered them in.

The three of them were sitting in the living room. Siti was already there, pouring them coffee. Both Marianna and Shahed were looking a little better than they were in the morning.

'Hi, guys,' I said.

I went over and hugged them both and sat down.

'Hope everything went well at the office?' I asked.

'Not really,' said Shahed. 'Everyone was shattered. Nobody could believe that Greg was gone. The whole office looked like there were zombies walking around.'

'Yes, Greg was such a nice person. Everyone knew him and he made sure he spent some time with each and every person, regardless of level,' said Marianna. 'Even Thevan, one of the building security guards was crying.'

'To add to the disruption, the four officers of the CID came to the office just after lunch,' continued Marianna. 'They spent time with Richard and also interviewed Sara, Greg's personal assistant. They also spent time in the pantry, and according to Sara, took samples of everything there.'

'Yes, and I overheard them saying that they were going back to Jocelyn's place later,' added Shahed.

'What are they doing with samples from the pantry?' I asked. 'I remember you saying that they focused on the kitchen at Greg's house too. What are they searching for and why?'

'They refuse to say anything or answer any of our questions,' Marianna said, with a trace of irritation. 'When Richard asked about the results of the autopsy, all the inspector said was, "We will let you know in due course, investigations are in progress."'

Something seemed off. The cause of death was quite apparent, I thought. What were the police looking for?

'Jocelyn is waiting for someone to tell her when they will release Greg's body,' said Marianna, 'only then can we start planning the funeral. Everything is in limbo,' she sighed.

While we were talking, I noticed that Shahed was sitting a distance away from Marianna. That was unusual. Didn't they usually sit together on the same sofa? I was not sure whether I was imagining things or whether Nysa's question from the morning was playing on my mind.

Nysa gradually steered the conversation to more pleasant topics.

Marianna and Shahed had planned to take a vacation to Europe later in the year, visiting Spain, Catalan, Portugal, France and Monte Carlo.

'Have you done the bookings for the trip?' asked Nysa.

Marianna looked at Shahed for a brief moment.

'Umm, the ticketing is done, but we are not sure if …' she said, haltingly.

'Yes, we are reconsidering the plan,' said Shahed, shortly.

'Oh, that is a shame,' said Nysa. 'You guys were so looking forward to this. You haven't had a break for a long time!'

'Well, we will see how it goes,' said Shahed, 'and what about both of you? You were planning to go to Bali next month. Is that on?'

'Of course,' said Nysa, 'we have done all the bookings. Daddy has booked a suite at the Alaya Resort, it is supposed to be beautiful.'

'Where is that, in Ubud?' asked Marianna.

'Yes, and we are also going to spend a couple of days in Nusa Dua, at the Marriott,' said Nysa.

'I wish I could go with you,' said Marianna, wistfully.

Shahed's phone rang. He excused himself and went out to the balcony to take the call.

Nysa arose.

'Let me see what's to be done for dinner,' she said, 'I think we are having biryani rice and dhal curry.'

Marianna got up, too.

'Let me help, Nysa,' she said, 'and I would like to have a quick wash before dinner, if that's okay with you.'

'Oh, absolutely,' said Nysa, as they walked towards the kitchen together.

I sat alone in the living room, awaiting Shahed's return.

Something was not right, I thought again. The reason for Greg's death was clear to anyone who looked at his face. This should have been a slam dunk for the police. Why were they searching kitchens and pantries?

As I pondered the unknowns, Shahed completed his call and came back into the living room. He sat beside me.

'All well?' I asked.

'Yes, a couple of issues that I have to sort out in the office,' he said, 'I was to go to Jakarta this week, but I have rescheduled the trip.'

'And otherwise?' I prompted gently.

He didn't respond. He got up abruptly.

'I need to use the restroom,' he said. 'Be back in a few minutes.'

I got up and collected the mugs, tray and bowls and took them to the utility area.

As I crossed the kitchen, Marianna came out, with her phone to her ear. She went into the living room, presumably to head to the balcony.

I rinsed the crockery and loaded the dishwasher.

Then, I wandered into the kitchen to see what, literally, was cooking.

Nysa and Siti were there, putting final touches to our dinner. The biryani smelled heavenly.

'Should I lay the table?' I asked Nysa.

She was just about to reply when Marianna burst in.

'He was poisoned!' she said excitedly.

Her words brought everything to an immediate halt.

She gathered herself.

'I just got a call from Jocelyn,' said Marianna. 'The CID Inspector was with her till half an hour ago. He informed her that Greg's cause of death was poisoning!'

Poison? How the hell did that happen? And when?

CHAPTER 29

Before we could respond, Marianna turned around.

'I need to tell Shahed,' she said, 'where is he?'

'He went to use the washroom,' I said.

'I'll just be back,' she said and disappeared.

Nysa and I looked at one another.

I remember telling you that we were major aficionados of crime and thriller fiction. We were also, in our youth, fans of Agatha Christie, Arthur Conan Doyle, Dorothy Sayers and Raymond Chandler. We loved reading and watching crime dramas of all genres.

This was the first time we had encountered anyone who was poisoned in real life.

Nysa stood wide eyed, the biryani forgotten. Her hand crept to the hollow of her neck, her go-to gesture when she was excited or alarmed.

'Poisoned?' she asked, her voice at least half an octave higher than normal.

Siti looked at both of us. She was not in the loop but realised that something momentous had happened. Siti is very wise. She said nothing. She picked up the biryani and went towards the dining room.

'Come, let's sit down,' I said to Nysa, 'I am sure Marianna will tell us more.'

Nysa and I walked into the dining room just as Marianna and Shahed did.

'… But he was killed in the club,' Shahed was saying to her, 'in the restroom, as we were first informed. How does poison fit into this?'

I gestured to them to sit at the table.

'Marianna,' I asked, when we had taken our seats, 'could you share what Jocelyn told you? In full?'

She took a deep breath.

'It seems Greg was poisoned. While having dinner with his client, he felt unwell and went to the restroom. There, he lost his balance, fell against the sink, hit his head and collapsed. That is why they first thought that he had died due to blunt force trauma, or that is the term Jocelyn used. But on doing the autopsy, they found traces of poison in his body.'

Her voice was wavering as she spoke and her eyes had filled. She was desperately trying to control herself.

'So, was he poisoned in the club?' asked Shahed, still coming to terms with this latest development.

'Jocelyn didn't say,' replied Marianna. 'I don't know whether the Inspector told her.'

'But,' interjected Nysa, 'if the police were looking for clues in Jocelyn's kitchen and then in the office pantry, they must have believed that the poisoning happened before Greg came to the club, right?

We eat at the club often, and it would have been reassuring to know that any poisoning happened outside, rather than in the club.

'I don't know,' said Marianna, tremulously.

'Could this have been an accident?' I asked. 'Could Greg have consumed something by mistake?'

'No,' said Marianna. 'Jocelyn said that the Inspector made it clear that this was homicide. Something to do with the poison being difficult to find or obtain, she said.'

'Poor Jocelyn,' said Nysa, 'this must be such a shock to her. First, she loses her husband, and then to find out that it is murder.'

'Yes, Jocelyn is completely lost,' said Marianna, 'she could never have imagined something like this happening. She and Greg were so happy together ...'

'Were they?' snapped Shahed.

All of us looked at him. He felt our stares.

'Sorry, but there is more to this,' he said. 'People don't get poisoned randomly. There must be something behind this incident ...' he trailed away.

'But who could do this?' asked Marianna. 'Greg was such a sweet person. Everybody loved him!'

Shahed muttered something under his breath. I was sitting next to him, and thought I heard, 'Some more than others'.

'I think we should have dinner,' said Nysa, evidently sensing the tension.

'Yes, I am starving,' I said, 'let me help Siti bring over the food.'

The biryani was hot but dinner had gone cold. Marianna barely touched the food, and Shahed seemed to be elsewhere.

Nysa tried to keep the conversation going but her attempts sputtered out like a damp candle.

'Does anyone want dessert?' asked Nysa, after we were done with the meal. 'Chocolate parfait?'

Usually such a question was received with much acclaim. Tonight, it collapsed like Nysa's early cakes.

'I would love one,' I said, to fill the silence.

Shahed stirred himself.

'Me too, Mom,' he said, 'thank you.'

The parfaits were delicious, as always. In a few minutes, Shahed had recovered from his earlier snit to put away two of them. Even Marianna, who started very listlessly, was licking her spoon by the end.

'It's best that we leave now,' said Marianna, when we rose from the table.

'Yes, I have a lot of work to catch up on,' said Shahed.

Both of them spoke at Nysa and me.

Nysa looked at me. I shrugged. I was not averse to their leaving, early as it was. I had some thinking to do.

We walked them to the door and exchanged our customary goodbyes and hugs.

After they had left, Nysa turned to me.

'Did you see,' she asked, 'there is something going on between Shahed and Marianna.'

I nodded.

'Yes, something is wrong,' I agreed. I did not tell her that I knew what it was.

'What can we do?' she asked, her voice strained.

'I don't think we can do anything till we know what the problem is, sweetheart,' I said, putting my arm around her. 'Anything we do may worsen the situation.'

She nodded, though not seeming convinced.

'Let me go and help Siti clear up,' she said.

'Yes, I need to complete some work,' I told her, 'I'll join in an hour or so.'

I traipsed to the study, closed the door and sat at my desk.

Wow, that was a lot to take in!

My first assassination, and I came in ... second?

I was almost offended.

But the more important questions were—who had poisoned Greg? And why? And when? And where?

(You will remember, these four questions, along with 'how', hold the secret to the meaning of life. And in this case, death.)

Could it have been Jocelyn? Did she know about Greg and Marianna? Poison is supposed to be a woman's go-to murder weapon, or so various true crime books and serials say. But Greg came to the club directly from the office along with his client. When could Jocelyn have had the opportunity? Unless it was some kind of delayed release poison that she had administered in the morning or the previous night.

Could it have been someone in the office? Another paramour, jealous of Greg's shifting affections? Who is to say that he was not having multiple affairs?

Could it have been the client? Was Greg in possession of incriminating information, and needed to be silenced? But the police seemed to have ruled the client out as a suspect.

Scores of questions swirled in my mind, one leading to or giving rise to another. Sadly, I was unable to muster any answers.

I needed to know more. I needed to find out more.

I took a deep breath and parked this issue aside.

There was another, more pressing matter to deal with. Lee Sun Wah.

The situation had changed completely. Greg had been poisoned. I was not the cause of his death. (At best, I was the cause of hastening his death). Lee had nothing to blackmail me with now.

Should I continue on my original path, or should I seek a more peaceable one? Should I close the deal or negotiate further?

I was planning to call him at 11 a.m. tomorrow. I had more than twelve hours to ponder and plan my approach.

I got up, turned off the light in the study, and went to join Nysa in bed.

Interlude 9 – Nysa, Suspicious

First, it was Ishmael and his strange behaviour.

Then, it was Shahed and Marianna and the distance and coldness between them.

Now, it is this Greg who has been murdered in broad daylight!

All this in two-three weeks?

Something is dubious about all this.

Every detective story I have read has advised me to mistrust coincidences.

Everything going well for years together, and suddenly, within the space of two weeks, our world turns upside down?

I don't think so.

And Ishmael's reactions over the past couple of days? Not real. He is putting on an act. I can read him better than he knows. I have lived with him for forty years! He definitely knows more than he is saying or showing. Even the other day, when I was talking to him about Shahed and Marianna, his reactions were slightly off. It was almost as if he was expecting to hear what he was hearing. Like a confirmation of something he already suspected or knew.

I am going to confront Ishmael. How dare he keep lying to me, his wife? How am I supposed to support him and help him if I don't even know what is happening? I am really angry with him, and I am going to make sure he knows it.

And Shahed! What is he doing? Marianna is in shock and grief, and he is behaving weirdly? This is not the Shahed we brought up. Doesn't he see that Marianna desperately needs him? Why is he acting so remote and stand-offish?

There is something that both of them know but are keeping to themselves. And I am going to find out what.

Should I call Marianna's father? Kabir is such a calm and cool person, maybe it will help Marianna if he comes and spends a few days with them.

Poor Greg and poor, poor Jocelyn. I can't imagine the horror she is going through. I hope her parents and family are with her.

I am going to give both Ishmael and Shahed a good talking to this week. And if they don't sit up and listen and obey, they will seriously regret it.

Should I ask Marianna and Shahed to stay with us for a few days? Just for a change of scene?

Gosh, I need to finish the research on the Vijayanagara wars and submit it by tomorrow. I have at least two hundred pages more of reading to do.

That Ishmael. Keeping secrets from me. I'm so irritated!

CHAPTER 30

'Hello, is that Mr Lee?' I asked.

'Good morning, Mr Dollah,' he responded, 'I am glad to hear from you.'

It was 11 a.m. and I had reached a decision on which approach to take.

I had not taken the decision in bed; I was exhausted and dropped off to sleep as soon as my head hit the pillow.

I took it, as I did most decisions, when on my run.

I don't know if you are aware, but as you run, the body releases a chemical called norepinephrine, which enhances mental focus. It also pumps endorphins into your body's system which increases your sense of well-being. Together, these help dispel the fog of subjectivity and allow me to think objectively and clearly.

For me, running is meditation in motion.

I had taken the decision by the time I turned back to retrace my steps. After that, it was only planning what to say.

After breakfast, I said goodbye to Nysa (she seemed a little distant this morning or was I imagining things?) and drove to Rajesh's office. I sat down in my chair in my usual cabin. I did not want to risk even the slightest chance of Nysa overhearing this call.

I leaned back in my ergonomic chair.

'Hello, Mr Dollah,' he said, when he heard my voice and greeting.

'Mr Lee, perhaps you have heard the news?' I asked.

There was a pause.

'What news?' asked Lee, cautiously.

'The police have determined that Mr Closier died of poisoning,' I said matter-of-factly.

Another pause, a longer one this time.

'No, I hadn't heard,' he said.

'Oh, the news is spreading around in the club,' I said, 'and they suspect that he was poisoned either at home or at his office.'

He did not speak.

'Perhaps you may want to confirm this news first hand?' I asked, politely.

'Even if you are right, Mr Dollah,' he said, his voice taking on a tinge of agitation, 'this does not change anything.'

'Oh, I thought it did,' I said.

'No, it does not. You were there when Closier died. I saw you. You did not take any action or report it to the police. This means you are an accessory to his death,' he said.

'I was in the restroom at that time, but I did not see Mr Closier,' I said, 'he must have died after I left.'

'No,' he said, firmly. 'If that was the case, you would not have entertained my request for a meeting. You would not have called just now.'

He was right.

'I felt it was polite to listen to what you had to say,' I responded, 'and I had promised you this call.'

His voice rose.

'Regardless, you were there, and my informing the police of that can cause you much trouble, Mr Dollah,' he said, rather stridently. Was that a note of panic I heard?

'Mr Lee, I am giving you an opportunity to do the right thing,' I said. 'You are trying to implicate an innocent man to achieve your ends. That is not just or fair.'

I was trying my best to give him a way out.

'No! You were there and I will inform the police if you do not give me my money!' he almost snarled.

I kept quiet for a few seconds.

'Okay, Mr Lee,' I said. 'Since I am not able to get you to see reason, I will give you the money, to avoid any unpleasantness. When and where would you like to meet?'

'Umm, anywhere you want, in a public place,' he said, his voice climbing down the register as he spoke.

I pretended to think.

'Should we meet at MacRitchie Reservoir tomorrow evening around 6.30 p.m.?' I asked, trying to sound as if I had plucked a location from the air.

Lee was evidently not an experienced blackmailer. He should not have accepted the first option given to him.

'Okay, that should be fine,' he said, probably wanting to ensure that I did not change my mind. 'Please bring the cash in 10- and 50-dollar notes.'

'Okay, tomorrow at 6.30 p.m.,' I said, 'I will be at the lowest level of the car park.'

'Thank you, Mr Dollah,' said Lee, reverting to his polite tone, 'I look forward to seeing you.'

I shut off the Oppo phone I was using. I took out the SIM card and cut it into two. I put the pieces in my pocket.

I packed my stuff and drove back home. As soon as I reached, I called out to Nysa and headed straight for the study. I placed my briefcase next to my desk, left the study and walked to the dining room. Nysa was at the dining table, working on a presentation on her laptop, while the TV played an episode of *The Crown*.

'Hi, sweetheart, just came back from work, but I need to step out for an hour or so,' I said, 'I will be back in time for lunch.'

'Okay,' she said, again seeming cold and distant, 'have fun.'

I wondered if I should stop and speak to her. I don't like Nysa being unhappy. *Later*, I told myself as I left our condo and walked to Lucky Plaza. I went to the Simba shop and after about 20 minutes in line, reported the loss of my phone and their SIM card.

'When did this happen?' the young gentleman in a bright purple t-shirt asked.

'Yesterday evening,' I said.

I asked them to cancel the card. They verified my identify, confirmed that I was the rightful owner of the SIM card and put the process into motion.

I asked for a receipt for the transaction. They frowned at me. Paper was passé, it seems. I insisted. Finally, a young lady stepped into a small room behind the counter, and then emerged with a piece of paper which had what I wanted.

I thanked them and left the shop.

I turned left and went to Orchard Central, to the M1 store and bought a pre-paid SIM card. I didn't think I would need it, but just in case.

I walked back home to Nysa and lunch.

Lunch was a coldish affair. The food was piping hot, thanks to Siti, but the servings were cold, thanks to Nysa.

'How is your research going, sweetheart?' I asked.

'Good,' was the terse reply. That was strange—Nysa never lost an opportunity to educate me on history.

'Is there anything I can help you with?' I tried again.

'Yes,' she said, briefly raising her eyes to mine, 'but not now. I will speak to you when I am free.'

Nysa was evidently pissed at me. But why?

After lunch and washing up, I headed to the bedroom for a nap.

That evening, at around 6 p.m., I asked Nysa if she would like to come with me for a walk to MacRitchie Reservoir.

'No,' she said, as tersely as at lunch, 'I am busy now.'

Still pissed.

I drove to MacRitchie Reservoir. I parked the car and walked the route I had on Monday morning. As we crossed 'my bench', I looked carefully to check that the bench was out-of-sight. It was almost invisible to anyone looking through the trees in the dusk. The sky was still light, but there were no street lamps or any illumination close by.

I crossed the spot and continued till I reached the end of the path after about two kilometres, then turned around to go back to the car park. This was our normal route, mine and Nysa's. Nysa refuses to walk more than 4 kilometres, claiming it to be cruel and unusual punishment.

The walk was beautiful and the lake was serene.

I hoped it would remain the same after tomorrow.

Walking back, I again examined the spot. I couldn't find any disqualifiers. I nodded in satisfaction and continued walking,

I reached home, showered and read for a while before sitting down to dinner. An episode of *Jeopardy* was on, limiting the conversation.

'How is the research going?' I asked, when we were finished, still trying to make amends for God knows what.

'Almost done, I have to complete my presentation,' said Nysa, as we were clearing our plates. She sounded a little better. 'I'll be with you as soon as I finish and send this off.'

'No worries, darling,' I said. I had work to do, too.

On the way to the study, I picked up some old copies of *The New York Times*. I dropped them on the couch.

I opened the laptop and quickly found out that fifty thousand dollars would weigh about two kilograms. I also estimated the size of the package.

I spent the next fifteen minutes cutting up the newspapers and arranging them into sheafs. When I had got the right size, I went to the kitchen. I used Nysa's weighing scale. The package was a little over two kilograms. Perfect.

I went back to the study and wrapped the sheafs in a thick reinforced envelope and taped it securely. I returned the remaining newspapers to their original storage and put away the package into my wardrobe, behind my shirts.

I opened the bottom drawer of the desk and picked out the chop sticks. They were in good shape. I returned them to the drawer and shut it.

I sat at my desk and reviewed my plan. Twice.

As I left the study, I remembered Bruce Lee's words— if you spend too much time thinking about a thing, you will never get it done.

Enough thinking and planning. Time for action.

CHAPTER 31

I woke up on Wednesday morning at 5 a.m.

As I age, I have noticed that sometimes I get up at strange hours, and then struggle to go back to sleep.

Today was not such a day. I woke up feeling fully refreshed and energised.

I rose from bed, quietly so as not to disturb Nysa, and tip-toed to the bathroom.

I brushed and washed, liking what I saw in the mirror—clear eyes and a calm expression.

I stepped out into the study and had no idea what to do next.

Is this how it's going to be from now on, I wondered? A sense of excitement, a feeling of anticipation, a thrum of energy?

Over these last three weeks I recaptured something that was missing since I retired. Actually, to be honest, something that was missing for much longer than that. A sense of purpose, a clear direction, specific goals to accomplish. Not for anyone else but myself.

Is this what self-actualisation was all about?

Is this what the great philosophers spoke about when exhorting us to follow the path of duty, and to resist investing in the outcomes?

I looked out of the bay window. The sky was a lovely shade of grey blue. Streaks of light were dappling the horizon. The dawn was mostly silent, except for the excited greetings of some early birds.

I sat at my desk.

I pulled out my notebook and read through the various entries of the past few days. I had not updated the most recent questions and actions. I picked up a pen and quickly caught up.

As I placed the notebook back in its place, I agreed with myself that I needed to destroy it as soon as possible. Some of what I had written was quite incriminating. The police would love to have such a document clearly framing the case against me.

I couldn't help it; I was always a 'to-do list' kind of person.

But I would destroy it. As soon as I was done.

Hopefully today.

That thought did not elate me as much I thought it would. I leaned back in my chair. Am I enjoying this too much? Planning and researching, tracking and executing? Or is it just about using one's skills honed over forty years in a different milieu?

Was my mind saying that I should continue doing this? Become a bona fide assassin?

I tossed the thought around and parsed it for a little while. It didn't offend. In fact, one could argue that there was a place for such a role in our society. So many offenders of different hues and stripes, and so few overseers.

I shook myself.

This is what happens when old men get up early and don't have anything to do, I thought, smiling.

But, as I got up, I knew that I was going to return to this exploration, and soon.

I donned my running gear. I sent a text message to Nysa's phone, telling her that I was going for my morning run. As I did, I told myself that I would need to find out what was going on with Nysa. Last night, she came to bed, turned away from me and went off to sleep. Without a kiss, or even a 'good night'.

I normally ran between 7 a.m. and 9 a.m., when the day was bright and bustling.

The semi-dark was a nice change. Streets were mostly empty and the steady metronome of my feet against the sidewalk was soothing. I ran past the National Library, marvelling as I did each time I passed it, turned into Beach Road and made my way to the Marina Barrage. I crossed over and continued to the ECP and then to Tanjong Rhu and along Kallang River.

As I made my way back to our condo, the sun made its presence felt. I looked at my watch. Fourteen kilometres. Not bad for an old man.

When I stepped into our apartment, I smelt eggs frying. What a wonderful aroma.

I walked through the dining room into the kitchen. Siti was doing her usual magic.

'Good morning, Siti. Is madam awake?' I asked.

'Still sleeping, sir,' she replied.

By the time Nysa woke up, I was showered and shaved and was completing the *NYT* crossword.

'Good morning, darling,' I said, when she showed up in the living room.

Nysa gave me a cool look.

'Ishmael, we need to talk,' she said.

Uh oh.

'Yes, dear,' I said, keeping the newspaper aside.

She sat on the sofa next to one I was sitting on, tucking her legs under her. She pinned me with her gaze.

'Why are you lying to me?' she asked, her voice calm.

Wow, I was not expecting that.

'What …' I started, my voice disgustingly squeaky, 'what do you mean?'

'You know what I mean,' said Nysa, 'you know something about what is going on, with Shahed and Marianna and this Greg person. And you are keeping it from me. Why?'

I collected my thoughts as quickly as I could.

'Nysa,' I said, in my most ingratiating tone, 'you know that I never lie to you …'

'Ishmael, that is bullshit,' Nysa cut in, 'you lie to me. You know it and I know it. I know you do it thinking you are protecting me or something. It is condescending and hurtful. I don't want your reassurances. I want the truth.'

Wow. It had been a while since Nysa had been so annoyed with me.

I sat forward.

'I am not lying to you, Nysa,' I said, lying. 'I know of certain things that are not mine to disclose or share. I find it difficult to keep these to myself but I have to.

'I need you to trust me on this,' I continued, my every pore oozing sincerity, 'and I promise that I will tell you everything I can soon.'

Nysa's face twisted.

'Are these things related to Shahed and Marianna?' she asked. 'Are they in trouble?'

'Yes, it is related to the children,' I admitted, weaving as persuasive a narrative as I could, 'but they are not in any trouble, per se. This I can assure you.'

'And why can't you tell me?' she asked, hurt evident in her voice.

'What I have is all hearsay and conjecture, Nysa,' I said, injecting distress into my voice, 'I myself don't know what is the truth and what is not.'

Nysa pondered my last statement.

'Should I talk to the kids?' she asked, finally.

'I think they need to talk to you,' I said, my one true statement in this conversation.

'Okay,' she said, and started to get up.

I rose and went to her.

'I am sorry,' I said, taking her hands, 'I hate to be in this position. I hate having you mad at me.'

Nysa squeezed my hands.

'I have to get to work,' she said. She ran her right hand across my cheek, and walked to her study.

I think that went well. Better than expected. Not yet back to normal but on the way.

The day passed quietly. There were no calls from Shahed or Marianna. Nysa stayed in her study and worked on her research; I read *The Economist* and started Rick Riordan's latest book.

We had a quieter than normal lunch. I told her that I had a meeting between 6 p.m. and 8 p.m. and shared with her the careful fabrication that I had put together. She seemed to accept it at face value. She looked at me a couple of times searchingly, but I didn't make much of it.

After lunch, we lay down and watched two episodes of *The Crown*. Nysa laughed at a couple of my comments. The Royal Family was very effective at inflicting damage on itself, I thought, as I nodded off for a brief siesta.

At 5 p.m. when I arose, Nysa was back in her room continuing her research. I went to the study and gathered everything needed for the evening's meeting. This included a pair of thin disposable nitrile gloves, a bunch of napkins, a couple of cloth rags and a disinfectant cleaning spray. I put all this into an old cloth tote bag along with the package of newspapers and the chopsticks.

I also took an unbranded black baseball cap and two N95 masks.

At 5.45 p.m., I said bye to Nysa and went down to our basement. At one corner of the basement, the condo management usually kept four or five orange traffic cones. I picked up two, put them in the trunk and drove down to MacRitchie Reservoir. I parked in the covered parking, got out and put on my cap and hung the mask over my ears and chin. I took the two traffic cones, put them in an Ikea bag and quickly walked to the spot that I had picked out.

There was no one there.

I did a quick recce. I removed the cones and placed them next to each other near the bench. In Singapore, traffic cones meant that there was work in progress. We are well conditioned here (to almost Pavlovian levels) to follow rules. No one would go past the cones and sit on the bench. I rolled up the Ikea bag and pushed it into the bottom of one of the cones.

I came back to the car park and sat inside the car and waited.

At 6.20 p.m., I saw a grey Benz drive in. It was Lee. He drove past my car and parked about 100 metres away.

I got out with the tote and moved three cars away and leaned against a white Corolla. In a few minutes, he came walking towards me, his head scanning both sides. He saw me and his stance visibly relaxed.

'Good evening, Mr Dollah,' he said, as he neared.

'Good evening,' I said.

I offered him the second N95 mask.

'It is best if we are not seen together publicly,' I said, leaning close to him, almost conspiratorially.

He picked up on my cue.

'Yes, yes,' he said, and wore the mask. I pulled up mine so that it covered my nose and mouth.

'Come,' I said.

He eyed my tote bag. He didn't say anything.

We walked, almost strolled, to the bench. By then, the sun had commenced its descent. The path we took was covered more in shadow than in light. By the time we reached, the sky was a dark metallic grey.

'Where are we going?' asked Lee, a little worriedly.

'Just here,' I said, as I shifted the cones and led him to the bench. 'I thought it best if we carried out our transaction in privacy.'

'Ah yes,' he said, 'very true.'

'Please sit down,' I said, as I sat on the left of the bench. He sat to my right.

'Before I hand over the money, how do I know that this will end here?' I asked. 'How do I know that you won't bring it up again?'

Lee was expecting that question. He drew himself up.

'I am a man of my word,' he said, with ridiculously ironic dignity. 'After this, we will consider this matter closed for ever. In fact, you will not see me again.'

'Really?' I asked, 'But we are both members of the club ...'

'I am selling my membership,' he said, 'I will probably move to Malaysia, Penang.'

'I see,' I said, nodding. 'Okay, I will accept your word as a gentleman.'

I reached into the tote bag and pulled out the package with the newspaper sheafs and handed it to him.

'Please open it, and count it,' I requested.

He grabbed the package and began to pry open the tape.

CHAPTER 32

The package was sealed with six layers of tape. I had at least three minutes.

I stood up, and as I did, I quietly slipped on the plastic gloves.

I stretched and grunted, to prevent any suspicion. Lee was too occupied in trying to remove the tape to suspect anything.

I picked up the two chopsticks and placed one in my right pocket and held the other in my right hand.

I turned left and left again, so that I was behind the bench. I positioned myself just behind Lee, about a foot to his left.

Lee grunted as he tore off the last piece of tape.

He opened the envelope. He put in his hand and pulled out the contents.

He saw the sheafs of newspaper.

'What is this?' he barked.

He turned his head to the left, noticed that I was behind the bench and swivelled upwards.

'You are cheating ...' he started, indignantly.

I bent down and held his chin firmly in my left hand.

With my right hand, I placed the sharpened end of the chopstick against the inner corner of his left eye and pushed hard.

The chopstick performed exactly as it had with the hard-boiled egg and the tomato and the grape. It slid in without reluctance.

Lee's body shuddered. His mouth opened in a gasp.

I kept holding his chin tightly.

I rotated the chopstick with my right hand, using the bridge of his nose as a fulcrum. This time, I met some resistance, but not much. I continued moving the chopstick in and out and around for about 15 seconds.

Lee's body suddenly relaxed and went limp.

I slowly pulled the chopstick out. It was wet. I let go of his chin and reached into the tote bag and pulled out some napkins. I placed them on the bench and kept the chopstick on top.

I peered at Lee. The evening had darkened by now, so I had to examine him quite carefully.

I looked at his left eye. Other than a little discoloration near the corner and a tiny spot of blood, there was no evidence of any disturbance. I took out two more napkins and dabbed the blood away carefully.

I closed his eyes. He seemed at peace. He was still sitting up, a little slumped, as if he were taking a nap.

I picked up the chopstick and using the napkins, wiped it clean. I wadded the napkins and threw them into the water.

I took both chopsticks and walked about twenty metres. I placed the first one, pointy end against the ground, and stepped on it. It sank in smoothly. I pushed hard till there was no sign of it anymore. Twenty metres further, I did the same with the other chopstick.

I came back to the bench, collected Lee's mask, the envelope, the newspaper, the napkins and the traffic cones. I pulled off my gloves after checking if they had anything on them and put everything into the tote. I placed the bag on the bench.

Then, I felt Lee's pockets and found his phone and pulled it out. It was an older model and needed only his fingerprint, which he kindly provided without demur.

I went into the call history and found the call that I had made from the Oppo phone. I deleted it and a few others, which did not have names, at random. Yes, I knew that the phone carrier would still have the records but at least it would not be obvious.

I placed the phone back in his pocket.

Stepping back, I looked over the scene once again, carefully.

All I could see was an elderly man, tired, taking a nap on a park bench.

He should have really taken the high road, I thought.

I picked up the tote bag and walked the long way around to the car.

Leaving MacRitchie Reservoir, I drove towards Bishan and parked outside the Ang Mo Kio park.

I pulled out the cones and left them in the boot. Then I carried the tote bag and walked in, still wearing my cap and mask.

I dropped the mask in one rubbish bin. I dropped the napkins and the gloves in another.

Then I went back to the car and drove back to Newton food court and parked.

I carried the tote bag in. I ordered a Bandung drink, and while sipping it, dropped the newspaper, the envelope, and rags in different bins. The tote was empty.

I went to the food court washroom. I rinsed the tote bag. Then, I discarded it and the empty Bandung glass in the rubbish bin.

Having completed all my tasks, I went back to the car, got in and drove home.

By the time I reached home, it was past 8 p.m.

'Hi Nysa,' I said, 'do you feel like a glass of wine?'

'You are looking cheerful,' she observed, 'I presume the meeting went well?'

'Oh yes,' I said, 'I closed the deal.'

'Then we must drink to that,' she said, smiling.

I poured her some rosé, and myself some red wine. We sat on the couch in the dining room, and I told her about how we had concluded a deal to sell my client's products across South East Asia at very advantageous terms.

We had a second glass each, and then moved on to dinner.

After dinner, we cleared the table, and I helped wash up, whistling as I did so.

Nysa looked at me appraisingly.

'You really are in a good mood tonight,' she said.

'Yes, why not?' I asked, smiling. 'A book of verse, a flask of wine and thou beside me,' I quoted the eternal Omar Khayyam.

She giggled.

'Sometimes you are quite ridiculous, you know, Ishmael,' she said.

'Yes, I know, and you love me in spite of that,'

'I do,' she said, and came and kissed me.

'Hold that till we are in our bedroom,' I said suggestively.

She raised an eyebrow and went back to putting away the dishes.

I went to the study.

I sat down on my chair and put my feet up on the settee.

Looking out at the cloudy sky, I reviewed everything that happened today.

I had ensured that there were no cameras where I had parked.

Lee and I met no one on our way to the bench.

All the collateral was disposed of thoroughly.

His phone was sanitised, sort of.

I had spoken to Rajesh and agreed with him that I was with him between 6.30 p.m. and 7.45 p.m. to discuss a sale agreement.

The only person who had really seen Lee and me together was the shop assistant at BreadTalk in Scotts Square. I doubt he would remember us.

The only concern was Lee's phone records. There was a call on his phone from my Oppo. I had reported the phone and SIM card stolen, but still. If there was a thorough investigation, that call could lead to me being asked questions.

Could I do anything about it? No. But next time (next time?) I need to use a phone that could not be traced back to me. Question: how does one find a 'burner phone' in Singapore.

Having completed the review, I took a deep breath. Some parts satisfaction, some parts exhilaration, most parts excitement that was a long way from subsiding.

I changed into my night clothes and went into our bedroom.

Nysa was in bed wearing a blanket and little else.

I smiled at her joyfully and shed my clothes.

We crested the summit twice.

Interlude 10 – Shahed, Betrayed

What a fucking terrible evening it was yesterday.

I thought it was just going be a couple of drinks with Nelson and Sugiman. Three colleagues travelling on work chilling together.

I could see that they were uncomfortable. That something was bothering them. The sudden glances. The dropped eyes. The solicitous enquiries.

And then, after much hemming and hawing, telling me about their visit to Nestor & Ross.

'You know the CMIG claim, Shahed,' Sugiman had said, 'the client had appointed Nestor & Ross to represent them.'

I had nodded. I knew this. But it was a legal issue and nothing to do with me.

'So, we were there for the preliminary fact-finding meeting,' Nelson had said, and described meeting the partner and two associates from the firm.

'I have known James for many years,' he continued, talking about one of the associates, 'we were associates together in Yeo & Moon some years ago.'

Sugiman took over from him.

'When the partner left the room,' he said, clearly distressed, 'this James Hong started talking about you and Marianna.'

And then, in fits and starts, there were all the ugly, heart-breaking details. And their sincere apologies for being the bearers of bad news. And the sympathy and pity on their faces.

How could Marianna do this?

I thought she loved me.

We've been together for almost twelve years.

She knows I adore her.

How could she do this?

That, too, with a lech like Greg. I remember her telling me that he was a predator, constantly hitting on women and having affairs. I remember her telling me that she felt so sorry for Jocelyn.

And she sleeps with the same bastard?

I am glad the son of a bitch is dead. He deserves to be.

How long has this been going on? Now I understand all the late meetings and the shutting of the laptop and the secretive phone calls. How could I have been so stupid and ignorant? How could I have missed all the signs?

I wish …

It's too late now.

There's no going back.

As soon as I get back, I am going to ask her for a divorce. Then she can go and sleep with anyone she wants.

How am I going to tell Mom and Dad? They love Marianna. They think the world of her. They are going to be so disappointed and disillusioned.

Oh Marianna.

Why?

What am I going to do without you?

Life fucking sucks.

CHAPTER 33

The next morning, once again, I woke up with the larks. At least I think they were larks. They may have been mynahs.

After my morning rituals, I went into my study.

First, I updated my notebook.

The lack of any immediate future tasks dampened my mood a little.

Then, I reviewed the previous day once again. No new insights presented themselves.

I sat in my chair, turned it to face the bay window and looked out into the gradually lightening dark.

I still had to figure out Greg's death.

Who could have poisoned him? And why?

The only probable suspect was Jocelyn. If she had found out about his dalliances, she may have decided that being a widow was better than being a scorned wife or divorcée.

But that was the obvious path. Occam's Razor is all very good, but humans are complex creatures and don't hew to the simple or obvious.

I examined the matter from as many angles as I could. I could not reach anything close to an outcome.

So I took a deep breath and parked the matter.

I changed into my running clothes and set out from the condo. Exiting the gate, I turned left and started towards the Botanic Gardens.

As I picked up speed, I started considering the situation between Marianna and Shahed.

Greg was gone. Would that be enough to salvage their relationship? Or was the crack too deep?

I knew Shahed suspected something. But did he actually know? In this case, wasn't ignorance bliss?

What would Marianna do? Mourn or repent?

These topics were not my forte. I would need to speak to Nysa and ask her to find a way to help the kids move on.

What next? Yes, I would need to inform Rajesh that I did not need his office anymore. My 'assignments' were done.

As I was compiling my mental checklist, I recalled the afternoon after Greg's death, when I had a minor epiphany about purpose and relevance.

These questions had been simmering in the back of my mind.

The last few weeks, I realised, I felt much more alive. Much more focused. Useful, actually.

Was an assassin's role akin to a CEO's role?

Both needed dispassionate analysis, detailed planning, precision execution and thorough review.

Both needed the ability to be objective, calm, focused, ruthless and methodical.

Both needed some suspension of morality, a willingness to do things that most would not, or could not do.

I had had fun as a CEO. It was great running companies, building them, turning them around, transforming them. Closing a deal—whether it was a sales contract or a merger or a divestment—was truly satisfying.

I have had fun the past three weeks. Assassination was so much like closing a deal.

Defining a goal, preparing the approach, collating the resources, planning the actions, executing (ouch!) them, reviewing the process and outcomes, closing the loop.

The only difference was that in case of assassination, only one party got to leave the room.

Did that bother me?

I examined that closely.

The answer was no. It did not. In fact, when I was a CEO, I often felt that many of the parties I dealt with did not deserve to leave the room. Unfortunately, the terms of my employment did not extend to terminating them, only to our discussions.

Interesting. I would need to continue this introspection.

The Botanic Gardens were gorgeous as always. Trees and birds, lakes and tiny meandering paths. Every time I came here, I left renewed. I stopped at the Swan Lake and absorbed the calm for a few minutes before continuing.

When I returned, I was feeling both uplifted and weary.

Nysa was at the dining table, having coffee and glancing through her phone.

'Good morning, dearest,' I said, bending down carefully to kiss her while not sweating over her.

She turned and kissed me hard.

'Such a wonderful night,' she whispered, conscious of Siti in the kitchen.

'For me, too,' I whispered.

'Let me rinse off and join you for breakfast,' I said, turning away.

'Ishmael, one minute,' said Nysa, 'Marianna called a few minutes ago. It is Greg's funeral this afternoon at 4 p.m. She wanted to know if we were available to come with her.'

'Why?' I asked. 'What about Shahed?'

'Oh, he left this morning for Jakarta,' she said, 'he's coming back tomorrow evening.'

'How can he leave Marianna at this time …' I started. I took a deep breath.

'What do you think, sweetheart?' I asked Nysa.

'I think she needs us, Ishmael,' she added, 'I feel we should go.'

I don't like funerals. Of course, I don't think anybody likes funerals other than funeral parlours and florists. I prefer weddings. Sadly, at my age, I find that I am going to more funerals than weddings.

'Okay,' I said, rather reluctantly, 'If you feel we should go, we will go.'

I went to the utility area, changed out of my sweaty clothes, rinsed and dropped them in the washing machine. Wearing a towel, I went to have my shower.

An hour later, feeling fresh, clean and well fed, I sat down to read the *NYT* and to tackle the crossword.

The morning passed slowly but contentedly. Vanilla, not Rocky Road.

Then there was lunch and a siesta.

By 3.15 p.m., Nysa and I were up and dressed in our most sombre clothes. Since retirement, I had stopped wearing formals, so all I had was black chinos, an old white shirt, and my only blazer. I don't think Nysa approved, but she stayed silent.

We left our condo and went to pick Marianna on the way to St. James' Church.

Nysa called ahead and Marianna met us in their lobby. She got in, greeted us and we drove to the church.

The funeral was hushed and poignant, as most funerals are.

The priest delivered the usual homilies. A few people, including Richard, Nestor & Ross' Managing Partner, went up to the podium and spoke about Greg and his near God-like qualities. I wondered if Marianna would speak but she stayed seated and was neither called nor volunteered.

I was quite bored. I hadn't even known Greg.

I looked around at the nearly full pews. We were in the fourth row, on the left. As I was scanning the room, I saw a few people I recognised from past parties and from dinners with Marianna's colleagues. I couldn't recall their names, though. They just seemed familiar.

Then, I spotted a familiar face. Someone I had seen recently. A middle-aged Chinese lady, sitting in the second row on the right, just behind Jocelyn and her parents. I could see her profile, that's all.

Where had I seen her? I racked my brain. Nothing.

I moved on and continued people watching. Most were surreptitiously scanning their phones. Some were having hushed conversations. Two were fast asleep.

As my eyes scanned back to the front, I noticed the Chinese lady fussing with her purse. She was either trying to push in or pull out her umbrella, and it was resisting her attention.

Ahh! I remembered. She was the lady who sat at the next table from Greg that night. The one who brushed past me rudely. I tried to visualise that night in the club. Hadn't I seen this woman do something with the food tray … the one that the waiter had left next to Greg's table?

I leaned towards Marianna, who was sitting subdued but dry-eyed.

'Marianna,' I whispered, 'who is that lady there in the dark grey jacket? The one sitting just behind Jocelyn's parents?'

Marianna looked at where I was nodding. She turned to me.

'That is Madam Hwa,' she said, 'she is Jocelyn's aunt and her godmother. How do you know her?'

'I don't know her,' I said, 'but it seems like I have seen her somewhere. What does she do?'

'I don't think you could have seen her,' said Marianna, 'she lives in Taiwan. She is a bigshot in their foreign service. I only know her because I met her at a Christmas dinner at Greg's home two years ago. Jocelyn told me that they were very close, even closer than Jocelyn was to her parents.'

'Okay,' I said, 'maybe I am mistaken. I am forgetting more and more nowadays.'

'Ishmael,' Marianna whispered back. 'You have the memory of two elephants. You never forget a thing!'

We turned back to looking mournful and dignified.

But I knew.

I knew who had poisoned Greg.

And if 'foreign service' meant what I think it meant, I better leave before she saw me and remembered where she had seen *me* last.

Assassins are people too. We can be afraid.

CHAPTER 34

Over the next few minutes, I engineered receiving a call. It was simple. I sent a text to an old friend, 'Hey buddy, it's been a long time. Let's have a chat when you are free'.

He called. I allowed the phone to flash a couple of times, making sure that Nysa saw it. She looked at me and shook her head.

He called again. Nysa's lips thinned. That happens when she is irritated. Mostly with me.

I sent him another message, '10 minutes please, will call back.'

As soon as the ceremony ended, I whispered to Nysa.

'I need to take this call, so sorry. I will be in the car.'

She did not respond. Nysa used silence as a very potent weapon.

As everyone stood up and started shuffling out of the pews, I excused myself with Marianna and made my way through the throng to the front doors and rapidly walked to the car. I sat inside.

I knew I had no way to prove it but Madam Hwa poisoned Greg. He was fine when he entered the club.

He was fine before he started eating his food. The food that she had done something to. Soon after, he seemed to feel ill.

I calmed myself. Was I extrapolating more than necessary? Could there be another explanation?

If so, why didn't she greet Greg when she was right at a table next to him? Why did she leave so abruptly?

My phone rang again. It was my friend. I took the call, and spent a few minutes catching up while my mind was churning with possibilities.

Just as we were ending the call, I saw Nysa and Marianna walking to the car.

I got out and opened the doors for them.

'Let's go home, Ishmael,' said Nysa, 'we are not going to the cemetery.'

'Oh, okay,' I said, quite happy to hear this.

'Marianna is spending tonight at our place,' continued Nysa.

'Oh, nice,' I said, as I started the car and drove out of the parking lot, away from Madam Hwa.

We reached our condo and went up to our apartment.

Nysa and Marianna were sitting together and talking softly. I didn't stop to enquire; I just wanted to get to my study.

I went in, closed the door, sat down and pondered.

After a few minutes, I opened my laptop, fired up a little-known browser and typed in, 'Madam Hwa, foreign service, Taiwan'.

The next few minutes were very revealing. They also confirmed that Madam June Hwa was fully capable of poisoning Greg and that he was far from her first victim. She was part of what is euphemistically known as the Operations Division, and was tasked with protecting Taiwan from enemies, within and without. She had been doing this for the better part of four decades. I could have delved further but who knew who was watching?

Madam Hwa was Jocelyn's godmother. She was unmarried and Jocelyn was her daughter in all but biology and name.

I shut the laptop down.

One mystery solved—the 'who'.

I could guess at the 'why'. Jocelyn must have shared her unhappiness at her husband's philandering ways with her godmother. Then, Madam Hwa had either bilaterally or unilaterally agreed that he must be punished with extreme prejudice. Given Jocelyn's reaction to Greg's death, I suspected that the decision was Madam Hwa's alone.

The 'what' was poison.

The 'where' was at the club, a few minutes before I assassinated Greg for the second time.

The 'how' was when Madam Hwa spent a few seconds alone with Greg's food just before it was served.

I felt a sense of relief. I hated unsolved puzzles. They keep gnawing at me and irritating me to no end.

Poor Greg, I thought. He was killed twice.

I changed into casual clothes and went to join Nysa and Marianna for a drink.

As I entered the living room, I saw Marianna sitting next to Nysa. She was sobbing. Nysa had an arm around her and was murmuring consolatory words.

Is she *still* crying for Greg, I wondered. How close had they become?

Nysa heard me enter. She turned and beckoned for me to sit down.

'Marianna, please tell Ishmael what you started to tell me,' she said, kindly.

Marianna sat up a little straighter and wiped her eyes. She took a couple of breaths.

'Shahed wants to leave me,' she said, tears pooling in her eyes.

'Mm-hmm', I said.

So all my efforts (and Madam Hwa's too) were to naught?

'He thinks I was having an affair with Greg,' she continued.

'Mm-hmm,' I said. Nysa patted her on the back, encouraging her to continue.

'How could he think that!' she burst out angrily, 'I love him. I have always loved him! I can't imagine being with anyone else!'

I sat up.

'Mmm, what gave him the impression that you are …' I asked.

'Some bastard in my office has been telling everyone that Greg and I are having an affair,' she said, 'and that has somehow reached Shahed. Then Shahed checked with the office and found that Greg and I have been going out of the office together some afternoons and concluded that I am cheating on him …' She started weeping again.

Nysa put an arm around her.

'And have you been going out with Greg?' I asked softly.

'Yes, Ishmael,' she managed, 'about three months ago, Greg and I had a chat. We were both unhappy in Nestor & Ross. We were bringing in the lion's share of clients and revenue but there was little or no recognition or reward.

'So, we decided that we should leave Nestor & Ross and set up our own firm,' she continued, dabbing her eyes, 'I was very excited, as this would mean that I would be name partner!

'We agreed to meet twice a week at a small hotel in Joo Chiat and work out the details. Greg found us two backers who would finance us and take a 25 percent stake in the new firm. They would also attend these meetings.'

I thought back to the day I saw Marianna and Greg exit from Hotel Wellcome. I recalled that they had been followed by two men in suits.

'We had completed everything—business plan, registering the company with ACRA, shareholders' agreement,' she explained. 'We had spoken to most of our clients who were very happy to go along with us. In fact, the evening that Greg died, he was meeting with one of the last few clients to entice him to come over to our new firm.

'Now Greg is dead, as is the new firm,' she concluded sadly. 'On top of this, Shahed hates me and wants to leave me.'

She turned her head into Nysa's shoulder and started weeping again.

You remember my telling you that I was an asshole? That I was arrogant and moody and annoying and tone deaf?

You can add 'judgemental' to that list. I jump to judgements and then act on them as if they were the gospel.

That is what I had done here. I heard two, saw two, and added them up to make twenty-two. And convinced myself that I was right.

'What were you planning to name your new law firm?' I asked gently.

'Closier & Dollah,' said Marianna. 'We had finalised office space in the CBD. We had given our business cards for printing. We were to get them this week. I was going to take Shahed out this Friday for dinner to our favourite restaurant and present him with my first card.'

Marianna looked woebegone, as if the world had collapsed around her. In all fairness, it had.

I clumsily stood up and went and sat on Marianna's right. I took her hand in both of mine.

'I am so sorry, Marianna,' I said, 'but Nysa and I will make things right. Shahed is being very silly. We will get him to see the truth.'

'How can he think that I would have an affair?' she cried, 'and that too, with Greg, who jumps into bed with anyone and everyone he sees! Why doesn't Shahed trust me?'

I cleared my throat.

'Marianna, men are essentially insecure beings. You are smart and beautiful and capable. I know Shahed loves you with all his heart but he is also worried that he doesn't deserve someone like you. This insecurity makes men do stupid things, nasty things and even terrible things.

'This is especially true when men are young. As they grow older, they gradually mature and learn to manage their emotions better. I know this because I have been there. When we were young, I would hate to see Nysa talking or laughing with another man. Insecurity leads to jealousy which leads to stupidity.'

Both Nysa and Marianna were looking at me wide-eyed.

I am rarely given to talking about emotions and feelings. They looked at me as if I had grown a third eye.

I got up, feeling quite embarrassed.

'As I said, we will set this right,' I said. 'Shahed is lucky to have you, and he knows it.'

Marianna smiled a tremulous smile.

'I am so lucky to have both of you,' she said and hugged Nysa.

I cleared my throat.

'Who was this colleague who has been talking about you?' I asked, causally curious.

'A nasty gossip called James Hong,' she said through gritted teeth. 'For some reason he dislikes me and finds different ways to put me down.'

'Mm-hmm,' I said.

Interlude 11 – Nysa, Reassured

Now I understand.

About Ishmael and his strange behaviour.

'I heard something when I was at the party,' he had said, when I confronted him, 'and I have been feeling hurt and angry since then.'

Why didn't he tell me, I asked.

'I was already miserable,' he had replied, 'What was the point compounding the misery? If it were true, what could you or I have done?'

There is no way it could be true, I had told him. No way Marianna would betray Shahed.

'You are an innocent, Nysa,' he had said. 'People do unexpected things all the time, and there are rarely explanations.'

So that is why he was lying to me. To protect me.

I love him so much. Orders of magnitude more than when we first met and fell in love. He can be a pain and an asshole but he has never let me down.

And Shahed.

Poor, dear Shahed, believing that his wife was cheating on him and not knowing what to do or whom to talk to.

Why couldn't he speak to me? When he was young, he would tell me everything. Now, I know so little about what he thinks or feels.

I need to sit him down and have a long chat. He needs to know that we are always here for him and always will be.

Poor Marianna.

She was planning to build a new career and company, and everything has gone topsy-turvy. Her prospective partner dead and her husband believing her to be unfaithful.

She needs us now more than ever.

I will speak to Kabir and ask him to come over next week if he can.

All these secrets.

They make everyone so miserable.

I hope Ishmael never keeps any more secrets from me.

CHAPTER 35

I sat with Nysa and Marianna for a few minutes, as Marianna gradually gathered herself.

It was almost time for dinner.

I excused myself.

'I will be back in a few minutes, ladies,' I said and went to the study.

I fired up my laptop and opened the ACRA Bizfile website.

I typed, 'Closier & Dollah' in the search bar.

It immediately spat out a result. Law Firm, it said, registered about a month ago. Four shareholders. The names matched.

I sat back.

Marianna was not lying. She had not been having an affair.

Had I made a mistake with Greg? Perhaps. But because of his philandering, he would still be dead. Madam Hwa would have assassinated him anyway. In one way, Greg had served a useful function—a practice target for me to develop my nascent skills on.

Rest in peace, I thought.

I opened my desk drawer and pulled out my notebook. On a fresh page, I wrote, JAMES HONG.

A feeling of savage excitement rippled through me. I added two more words.

My name is Ishmael Dollah.

I am sixty years old.

I am an assassin.

Segue 4 – Ishmael's Notebook

__ November:

Task 1:
~~To confirm the allegations.~~
    ~~1.   How can I confirm the allegations?~~
    ~~2.   What resources do I have at my disposal?~~
    ~~3.   What tactics best fit this situation?~~
DONE.

Task 2:
~~To separate Marianna and Greg.~~
    ~~1.   How do I find out everything about Greg?~~
    ~~2.   Where and how do I accost / confront him?~~
    ~~3.   What approach would ensure a permanent separation~~
    ~~between him and Marianna?~~
DONE.

Task 3:
~~Lee San Wah — to mitigate threat~~

1. ~~Is he a concern or a problem?~~
2. ~~What is the best approach?~~

DONE.

New Task:

James Hong—to terminate.

Epilogue – Greg Closier's Residence

She closed the lid of the suitcase and zipped it.

Her car would be here in half an hour.

She sat at the dressing table and looked in the mirror. She looked satisfied, she thought.

She felt satisfied.

Her Jocelyn was safe now. That hateful husband of hers could cause her no more hurt.

I had told her not to marry this ang moh, she thought. He was always a little too confident, a little too full of himself.

I had foreseen this. I wish I had acted then.

But Jocelyn was head over heels in love with Greg.

'You know, Aunt June,' she had said, in that sweet way of hers, 'he is such a darling. So kind and chivalrous and caring.'

All men are, my dear, she had wanted to say, when they want to bed you.

The first couple of years of their marriage had been all sweetness and light. Jocelyn was so happy. She remembered questioning her instincts. Had she been wrong about Greg?

And then, the first call a few years ago.

'Aunt June,' Jocelyn had sobbed, 'Greg is cheating on me. He is having an affair with someone's wife.'

She had flown to Singapore immediately to be with her goddaughter. To console her, to support her.

Do you want a divorce, she had asked.

'No, Aunty, I love him too much,' was the answer, 'and Greg is sorry. He said this was a mistake and he will never do it again.'

Ha.

Then the second call, and the third.

Each time, she could feel Jocelyn's broken heart, her shattered aspirations, the dullness in her eyes gradually becoming permanent.

Last week, another call.

Enough, she had said to herself. Greg was killing Jocelyn with a hundred cuts of betrayal and shame.

This time, when she flew to Singapore, she came prepared.

She could have contracted the job. She knew a dozen operatives who could have killed Greg without a second thought.

But this was personal. This was for her goddaughter and for all the indignities Greg had heaped on her, may the bastard burn in hell for eternity.

She got up and hefted the suitcase off the bed.

She felt a little tired.

It had been more than fifteen years since her last operation in the field. In Seoul, she remembered. The drug kingpin who thought he was going to make a fortune from her country. He had died by overdose of the very drugs he sold. She smiled.

Jocelyn was grief stricken now but she would be okay. The police were largely done with their investigation. The ceremonies and formalities were complete. Jocelyn would heal in time. She would be fine.

Madam Hwa pulled the handle out and wheeled the suitcase to the door.

Afterword – Closing A Sale

By now, having read my narrative so far, you should have grasped the principles of closing a sale.

It is not rocket science.

We start with defining our goal—what is it that we want to achieve.

Then, we map out the playing field—understand the ecosystem and its components, its drivers, its idiosyncrasies.

Next, we plan and decide our approach.

Once the approach is clear, we plan the resources needed—information, expertise, tools, processes, people, infrastructure.

Now that we have our goal, our framework, our approach and our resources.

It is time to prepare.

We prepare, then we continue to prepare, and finally prepare some more. Once we have completed this, we prepare again.

We review our preparations.

Then, we prepare to act. While we are doing so, we keep in mind President Eisenhower's famous words, 'Plans are worthless, but planning is everything.' The scenarios envisaged may never come about but our planning prepares us for scenarios that we did not plan for.

If everything goes according to plan, great.

If it doesn't, we are not stymied. We take the first opportunity that comes and execute.

We close the sale.

However, a closed sale is not necessarily a done deal. It can be undone in the immediate aftermath.

Sometimes, issues arise. External factors intrude. We need to keep a close watch.

If there is any sign of unravelling, we must act quickly and decisively to seal the breach.

We review our preparation, our execution, our post-execution actions.

When the ecosystem stabilises in its new configuration, we are done.

The sale is closed.

Sometimes, very rarely, the sale does not deliver the outcome you hoped or planned for.

That's okay. That's life.

Don't waste your time on regrets. Move on.

There is always another sale to close.

Failure is never fatal. Success is never final.

Except if you are an assassin.

Acknowledgements

Writing a book is sheer joy. Thoughts and words flood your mind and rush onto the screen in a deluge, faster than you can type. Sentences pool into chapters, which flow into one another, sometimes in trickles, often in torrents. You are careful not to be swept away, keeping your eye on the cadence and the rhythm that accompanies the flow. As you career past banks and shoals, you are always conscious of your source.

Of your parents who introduced you to the joy of storytelling.

Of your kindergarten and primary school teachers who helped you make sense of those black marks on white pages.

Of your first authors who reeled you in, welcoming you into a world of imagination and delight.

Of those special books whose words hammered and twisted and annealed your mind and soul.

Of every book that pulled you away from dreary reality into a different universe rife with possibilities.

Thank you, to all of you.

You have made the world extraordinary.

May your tribe increase.